PUFFIN BOOKS

The Silent Enemy

Dan Lee spends his time travelling between Asia and Britain. A wing chun master, he also trains in kickboxing and ju-jitsu.

With special thanks to Brandon Robshaw

TANGSHAN TIGERS

The Silent Enemy

Dan Lee

PUFFIN

Robshaw

Published by the Penguin Group
Penguin Books Ltd, 80 Strand, London WC2R ORL, England
Penguin Group (USA) Inc., 375 Hudson Street, New York 10014, USA
Penguin Group (Canada), 90 Eglinton Avenue East, Suite 700, Toronto, Ontario, Canada M4P 2Y3
(a division of Pearson Penguin Canada Inc.)
Penguin Ireland, 25 St Stephen's Green, Dublin 2, Ireland (a division of Penguin Books Ltd)
Penguin Group (Australia), 250 Camberwell Road, Camberwell, Victoria 3124, Australia
(a division of Pearson Australia Group Pty Ltd)
Penguin Books India Pvt Ltd, 11 Community Centre, Panchsheel Park,
New Delhi – 110 017, India
Penguin Group (NZ), 67 Apollo Drive, Rosedale, North Shore 0632, New Zealand
(a division of Pearson New Zealand Ltd)
Penguin Books (South Africa) (Pty) Ltd, 24 Sturdee Avenue, Rosebank,
Johannesburg 2196, South Africa

Penguin Books Ltd, Registered Offices: 80 Strand, London WC2R ORL, England

puffinbooks.co.uk

First published 2008
1

Series created by Working Partners Ltd, London
Text copyright © Working Partners Ltd, 2008
All rights reserved

The moral right of the author has been asserted

Set in Bembo
Typeset by Palimpsest Book Production Limited, Grangemouth, Stirlingshire
Made and printed in England by Clays Ltd, St Ives plc

British Library Cataloguing in Publication Data
A CIP catalogue record for this book is available from the British Library

ISBN: 978-0-141-32286-5

www.greenpenguin.co.uk

Mixed Sources
Product group from well-managed
forests and other controlled sources
www.fsc.org Cert no. SA-COC-1592
© 1996 Forest Stewardship Council

Penguin Books is committed to a sustainable future
for our business, our readers and our planet.
The book in your hands is made from paper
certified by the Forest Stewardship Council.

CONTENTS

Chapter 1

RETURNING HOME

Matt peered through the window at the soaring skyscrapers of Beijing, glittering in the sunlight. The view tilted as the plane banked and he felt a gush of relief as the wheels of the jet touched down with a bump. The plane taxied along the runway, gradually decelerating.

Matt loved flying – but this flight had been tense. He stole a look across the aisle at Andrei Drago, sitting alone. Drago caught Matt looking at him and gave a mocking smile, before turning away.

Shawn nudged Matt. 'He gives me the

creeps, that guy.' Shawn Hung was a member of the Tangshan Tigers, a secret gang Matt had set up with his friends. Along with Olivier Girard and Catarina Ribeiro they had first cracked the mystery of a missing jade dish. Since then they'd solved more than their fair share of crimes. But the big secret about the Tangshan Tigers was that they were just that – a secret. No other kids in the Academy knew the gang existed.

'I don't understand why he's here at all,' said Matt in a low voice. 'It's been bugging me all through the flight.'

'I know. He tried to knock out a whole roomful of people with sleeping gas, all because he was sore about being left out of the martial arts team –'

'And then Chang says he can transfer to the Beijing Academy!'

'He oughta be sitting in a police cell,' said Catarina, twisting round from the seat in front.

'Not being flown by private jet to one of the best schools in the world!'

'I suppose Chang must have a good reason,' said Olivier. 'He usually does.'

'Can't figure out what it is, though,' said Matt.

The plane's speakers emitted a soft, musical bong and the illuminated signs came on: YOU MAY UNFASTEN YOUR SEATBELTS.

'This way!' said Mr Figgis, the history teacher who had accompanied them on their trip. 'Two straight lines, please, two straight lines!'

The Tangshan Tigers gathered up their belongings and prepared to join the queue. Drago pushed past, making Catarina and Olivier fall back into their seats.

'Hey, quit pushing!' said Catarina.

'If you don't stand in the way, you won't get pushed,' said Drago. He gave a toss of the head and pushed past others down the aisle. Matt

3

could hear people tut loudly all the way down the plane.

'He's a charmer, isn't he?' said Olivier.

Catarina clenched her fists. 'I've a good mind to –'

'Forget it, Catarina,' said Matt. 'He wants to wind you up – don't let him.'

'You give good advice, Matt. The simple fish snaps at the bait, but the wily old carp is too wise.'

It was the voice of Chang Sifu, their coach. Matt turned and saw him standing behind them – a slim figure of medium height, with lightly silvered hair, wearing the kingfisher-blue jacket he favoured when not in martial arts costume. His face was calm as usual, but he radiated a sense of controlled energy.

He motioned them towards the exit. 'Time to leave; we are last.'

At the top of the steps, Matt paused to survey the scene before him: the wide expanse

of the airport tarmac, the glinting towers
of Beijing in the distance. It was good to be
back.

The rest of the students, led by Mr Figgis,
were already halfway to the arrivals building.
At last Matt had the chance to talk to Chang
Sifu.

'Sifu?' he said respectfully as they walked
across the tarmac. 'We don't understand –
could we ask you . . .'

'You may ask what you wish.'

'Well, about Andrei Drago – how come . . .?'

'How come he's joining our school?' said
Catarina bluntly. 'The guy's crazy!'

'Trying to knock out a whole roomful of
people! It could have been dangerous,' said
Shawn.

Chang inclined his head. 'But fortunately
danger was averted,' he said. 'Thanks to you.'

'Yes, but –' Matt hesitated, unsure how to go
on.

5

Olivier stepped in. 'We know there's a good reason why you couldn't stop him coming to Beijing,' he said. 'But we can't work out what it is.'

'It is not a question of what I could or could not do,' said Chang. 'It is a question of what is wise.'

'But why's it wise to let him in?' asked Catarina. 'I don't get it.'

Chang regarded all four of the Tangshan Tigers gravely. Then he said: 'Sometimes it is best to embrace enemy and make him your friend.'

Matt didn't want to show Chang Sifu any disrespect, but he couldn't help the question that came next. 'But why?' he asked, frowning. 'What he did was terrible.'

Chang Sifu raised his eyebrows and nodded. 'That is true. But there are reasons people do terrible things. We all deserve a chance in life. Look at you, Matt. Your instructor in London told you that the standard at the Beijing Academy team might be too high for you.'

Matt gasped. How did Chang Sifu know about that?

'But I gave you a chance to try out and you proved yourself. Drago just needs his own chance to prove himself. We should give it to him.' He glanced past the Tangshan Tigers at the rest of the team. 'The others are waiting,' said Chang gently. 'We must hurry.'

They caught up with the group in the arrivals building, collecting their luggage at the baggage carousel. Matt couldn't help eyeing Drago, wondering what he was thinking. Drago held his hand up, making the 'L' for 'Loser' sign at Matt. Then he smiled, picked up his holdall and turned his back.

Matt forced himself to take his own advice and not get wound up. 'Well – Chang must know what he's doing,' he said quietly to the other Tigers as they were boarding the luxury, air-conditioned, double-decker coach that would take them back to the Academy. 'He always does.'

'Yeah,' said Shawn. 'We've got to trust him.'

'It's one thing to trust Chang,' said Catarina. 'But I don't trust Drago.'

'We'll keep our eyes on him,' said Olivier.

'We'll watch him like hawks!' said Matt.

The coach doors swished shut behind them as they climbed aboard.

The following morning, the martial arts squad gathered for their training session at the *kwoon* – a spacious hall with matting on the floor, high windows and smooth, white light-panels on the walls and ceiling. One wall was decorated with paintings of scarlet dragons. All eleven of them – Matt, Shawn, Catarina, Olivier, Carl, Lola, Wolfgang, Abdul, Dani, Jahmal and Vincent – were there early. *There's*

nothing like victory in a tournament, thought
Matt, *to make you eager to train*.

As they waited for Chang, the Principal, Mr
Wu, popped his head into the room. To Matt's
surprise, Andrei Drago was with him.

'Well done, well done!' said the Principal.
Despite the early hour he was clad in his usual
well-cut dark suit and tightly knotted tie. Matt
sometimes wondered if he slept in this outfit.
'A famous victory – we certainly showed those
Kyoto chaps how to do it! And just in time to
appear in next year's school prospectus; what
very good timing! Now, I have brought the
new boy, Andrei Drago – you have met already.
I feel sure you will make him welcome!'

He ducked his head out of the door and
Matt heard his heels clicking away down the
corridor.

'What are you doing here?' Catarina asked
Drago. 'You're not in the squad.'

'I know; I have come to see if I can try out

9

for it,' said Drago softly. His manner was subdued, nothing like the blustering performance of yesterday.

At eight o'clock on the dot Chang Sifu opened the door. *He doesn't seem surprised to see Drago*, Matt thought. But then, Chang very seldom seemed surprised by anything.

'Sifu – could I try out for the squad, please?' asked Drago.

Chang Sifu regarded Drago thoughtfully. 'Are you prepared to work hard?'

'Oh yes, I am! I will work as hard as you ask me –'

'Well, squad,' said Chang. 'What do you think? Should we let him try out?'

No one said anything. *What are we supposed to say?* Matt wondered. It seemed ridiculous to let a loose cannon like Drago anywhere near the team – but now that he was a student at the Academy, he had as much right to try out as anyone else. 'Yeah, let him try out – why

not?' he heard himself saying. He saw
Catarina's jaw drop open.

Chang nodded. 'Very well. It is only fair to
give you a chance. 'You may train with us
today. If – and only if – I am impressed with
what I see, I will consider revising squad. This
depends entirely on what you can do.'

Andrei brought his hands together in front
of his chest as though praying, and bowed low.
'Thank you,' he said. 'Thank you very much,
sir, I will do my best.'

Matt felt a twinge of guilt for having been
so down on Andrei before. He'd done
something dreadful in Kyoto, but he seemed a
different person today. All that pushing and
face-pulling yesterday – could that just have
been bravado?

'Chang Sifu's giving him the benefit of the
doubt,' Matt whispered to his friends. 'Perhaps
we should too.'

Master Chang ushered them into place.

'Begin with simple stretching exercises to loosen muscles,' said Chang. 'Start with thigh-stretch, like so. Work in pairs.'

Matt was paired with Catarina.

'You don't really want Drago in the team, do you?' demanded Catarina as they went through the first routine together.

'Not really,' Matt admitted. 'I'm not sure he'll get in anyway. He wasn't good enough for the Kyoto team. But everyone deserves the opportunity to try out.'

'Form into two lines,' said Master Chang, interrupting them. 'Today we learn new and very important technique. You will need to concentrate.'

'Hey, give us a break!' said Carl. 'After the Kyoto tournament we deserve to take it easy!'

Everyone knew Carl for his loud mouth and arrogant opinions. His ego always got the better of him after a win, so it was no surprise that he had something to say today.

'Martial arts fighter should never take it easy,' said Chang Sifu.

'No, but I mean, we won the tournament, or maybe I should say, *I* won the tournament, so –'

'So I should immediately be made emperor of the whole world!' said Olivier, imitating Carl's accent. 'Emperor Carl the First, that's me!'

There was a burst of laughter. Matt always enjoyed Olivier's brilliant imitations of Carl. The only person who didn't enjoy them was Carl. He glared at Olivier through narrowed eyes. Olivier smiled back.

Chang held up his hand for calm. 'Focus of today's training will be on balance,' he said. 'You will learn to master your centre line.' He paused to let these words sink in. 'Does anyone know of concept of centre line?'

Matt racked his brains. Centre line? He saw Shawn raise his hand.

'I know a little bit about it. My grandfather

13

did wing chun, and he taught me – I don't know much, just the basic idea.'

Chang Sifu nodded. 'Tell us what he taught you.'

Shawn walked to the front of the mat so that all his teammates could hear him.

'The centre line is the area right in front of your body, right? And you have to focus on it, direct all your energies on it. Kind of point your whole body at it. And you've got to be balanced – have a good foot-base. If you've got a firm base to strike out from and you focus on the centre line, you should beat your opponent to the punch – because a straight line is the shortest distance between two points.'

As Shawn talked, Chang Sifu walked slowly back and forth behind him, listening.

'That is correct,' he said. 'Balance is the key. What this means in practice is –'

'Hold on!' protested Carl. 'This isn't fair –

it's biased to people who do kung fu. I do karate, it's not gonna suit my style –'

'It's not a question of styles,' said Chang patiently. Matt liked the cool way he put Carl in his place, never getting wound up by him. 'We are concerned only with what works best. You will find centre line theory can be applied to all fighting styles – it will make your karate techniques more effective if applied properly. You will also find this principle works not just in tournament but in real-life fighting situation. In street fight it is devastating.'

Matt blinked in surprise. He had never heard Chang talk of real fights before. He knew that Chang himself was awesome in a real fight – he had seen him in action against Sang and his henchmen under the Great Wall of China – but in the *kwoon* he always talked of martial arts as if they were just that – arts. Why was Chang talking about street fights? Matt glanced at the other Tigers. Catarina raised her eyebrows. Shawn frowned. Olivier pulled a 'search-me' expression.

'Adopt this stance,' said Chang. He stood with his legs apart, one foot about a shoulder's width behind the other. His knees were very slightly bent. 'Note that most of my weight is resting on back foot. Note also that toes, knees, hips, shoulders, all point in same direction: forward. Everything focused on narrow area in front of me.'

The students slowly adopted the same stance, as Chang went round adjusting a knee here, an elbow there. Matt found it strange and slightly uncomfortable – as a tae kwon-do practitioner, he was used to standing side-on to an opponent, protecting vulnerable areas. This stance made him feel exposed.

'centre line is narrow area directly in front of you. Imagine an enemy facing you: the centre line goes through his body, and that is where you must attack. If correctly centred, all your *chi*

– your energy – runs right up through your body, starting from back foot where your weight is placed. You will strike with great force, all your *chi* converging on the target. If channelled properly, you will punch harder than you ever thought possible. If attacked by multiple enemies, they need to be taken out fast. Before they have opportunity to co-ordinate. Go to meet them, intercept, hit them *bang bang bang*, using centre line. Strike hard, strike straight – control angles. Throw them off-balance and the fight is yours.'

Multiple enemies? Members of the squad glanced at each other uneasily.

Matt would never normally question Chang Sifu, but it felt strange to hear Chang talking about enemies in this way. 'Sifu, why are we changing our training?'

Chang gazed past Matt at an open window in the *kwoon*. Matt glanced over his shoulder and saw the Beijing landscape spreading out beyond the Academy.

'Your life does not begin and end in this *kwoon*, Matt. Nor does your training,' said their teacher.

'What does he mean?' Catarina whispered.

'What I mean,' said Chang, turning to Catarina, 'is that I want you all to be able to defend yourself wherever life takes you. I won't always be by your side.'

'Why? You're not leaving for another job, are you?' asked Carl Warrick. 'That would be totally unfair!' Trust Carl to put himself first. But Matt felt his own chest tighten at the thought of Chang Sifu leaving them.

Chang shook his head and smiled. 'I will never willingly abandon you.'

'Good,' said Carl, turning away. 'My father paid good money for me to be trained by you.' Matt gazed after Carl in disbelief. Was that boy for real?

'Time to practise control of centre line,' said Chang, ignoring Carl's last comment.

'Six of you to far end of *kwoon*, please.'

Matt was among the six who moved to the far end. He noticed that their white mat had been ruled with faint yellow lines of chalk, like the lines on a running track. Each lane was no more than fifty centimetres wide.

'Stand in lane and face opponent at other end,' said Chang. Matt looked down the lane and saw Olivier facing him, some twenty-five metres away. 'You must advance and face off – spar with opponent, attempt to drive back. You may use any style but you must concentrate on centre line. All attacks to be concentrated on that narrow area in front of you. You will stay inside your lane. Failure to do so will result in punishment – to run thirty times round perimeter of *kwoon*!'

He clapped his hands. 'Begin.'

Matt advanced. In the lanes to either side of him he was dimly conscious of the other students advancing as well, but he had eyes only for the looming figure of Olivier. It seemed strange to advance in this way, his whole body facing Olivier; he had to fight the temptation to turn side-on.

They closed. Matt parried a kick from Olivier, countered with a spear-hand thrust, which was blocked. He and Olivier knew each other's styles well and were evenly matched. For a while neither gained any advantage. Matt felt hemmed in, not being able to move outside the lane and vary the angle of attack. Then he saw that Olivier had left his side exposed; Matt swept his foot in a roundhouse kick aimed at Olivier's ribs. Olivier saw it coming and blocked hard. The impact made Olivier step back, but Matt was also thrown off-balance.

'Matt!' said Chang sharply. 'You breached centre line, your foot went outside your lane.'

'But –'

'Thirty laps!'

'Bad luck!' whispered Olivier.

It seemed harsh. After all, Matt hadn't actually stepped out of the lane, merely allowed his foot to stray outside it. But he didn't complain. He set off on his thirty laps.

Matt wasn't the only one to struggle with the centre line. He was soon joined by others running laps. First Wolfgang, then Lola, then Abdul, then Olivier, who had been re-matched with another partner, then Drago. Though Drago was no slouch, Matt had noticed while running his laps – he held his own against Shawn for a long time. But Shawn was adept, maintaining his balance on the back foot, never looking like straying outside the lines, striking hard and fast. After Drago, Shawn got the better of Catarina and then Carl, and by the end of the session he was the only student who had not been awarded the thirty-lap penalty.

Everyone was exhausted.

'No more face-offs today,' announced Master Chang. 'Session is nearly finished. We will finish with forty press-ups. Go!'

Matt groaned and threw a glance at the other Tigers. He lowered himself to the mat and began the press-ups. One . . . two . . . three . . .

'What's with Chang then?' asked Catarina. 'He's never given us a session like that before.'

'I know!' said Olivier. 'Did you notice he kept talking about "enemies", not "opponents"? And street-fighting situations? What's that all about?'

The Tangshan Tigers had gathered in Shawn and Olivier's room in the recreation hour after supper.

'And why did he work us so hard?' said Catarina. 'Face-offs, punishment laps, press-ups – I feel like I've played a football game, run a marathon and gone ten rounds in a boxing ring!'

'He wouldn't be doing this if he didn't think it was necessary,' said Matt. 'We know by now that Chang's always got a reason for what he does.'

'But what on earth can it be?' said Olivier.

'Could it be something to do with Drago?' said Shawn. 'Maybe Chang's expecting him to pull another stunt, wants us to stay sharp in case we have to spring into action again? Chang is taking a risk giving him a second chance.'

'Could be . . .' said Matt doubtfully. He hoped Shawn was right, that it was no more than that. Yet the explanation did not seem quite convincing. If that was the case, why train the whole squad in this way, since it was only the Tangshan Tigers who knew what a threat Drago could be? Why train Drago himself? And besides, why should the four of them need this kind of training to be prepared for whatever Drago might do? Drago was

23

sneaky and devious, but they could handle him in a fight without needing to know the centre line theory.

There was something else, some danger Chang foresaw, that he could not or would not warn them of at this time. Chang Sifu had said he'd never *willingly* leave them. So would he be forced to? Danger was lurking, Matt felt sure of it. And this time the Tangshan Tigers might have to face it on their own.

A NEW COACH

The sun was shining through the high windows
of the Beijing International Academy as Matt
and the Tangshan Tigers made their way to the
kwoon for early training the next day.

'Do you reckon we'll do more of that
centre line training today?' asked Catarina.

'I hope so,' said Shawn. 'I could get into
that.'

Matt was feeling better about things this
morning. Chang Sifu was putting them
through some extra-hard training. What
was so sinister about that?

Drago was waiting at the door of the *kwoon*. He was in his martial arts suit, leaning against the wall. He gave a nod to the Tangshan Tigers. Matt nodded back, though he wasn't sure whether Drago's greeting had been friendly or sarcastic.

'Still with us then?' said Catarina.

'Master Chang said I could continue to train with the squad.'

'Here we are again, guys!' came Carl's loud, brash voice. 'I wonder what crazy nonsense Chang's got lined up for us today – maybe he wants us to fight with our hands tied behind our backs, or –'

'The centre line theory is not nonsense!' said Shawn.

'Well, I wouldn't expect you to criticize your lord and master,' said Carl sarcastically. 'I tell you what, though, at least he made us work out yesterday – all those press-ups. At last the old man's making us break a sweat, and about time too!'

A New Coach

It was nearly eight o'clock. Lola, Wolfgang and Dani arrived, and shortly afterwards Abdul, Jahmal and Vincent. Master Chang expected everyone to be on time. He was often there well in advance of the students, meditating and exercising alone, and always opened the door to them at eight on the dot. But today eight o'clock came and the door remained closed. *Strange*, thought Matt. He peeped through the glass panel in the door.

'Can't see him,' he reported.

'Do you think he's OK?' said Lola.

'Maybe he had to go and see Mr Wu about something,' suggested Catarina.

'Or maybe he's all tired out after yesterday!' said Carl. 'He is getting on a bit, after all.'

'Yeah?' said Shawn. 'I bet you couldn't keep up with him at any exercise!'

'I bet I could!'

'Right!' said a loud, deep voice, making them all jump.

A tall, broad-shouldered man with a muscular build stood before them, his chin thrust forward aggressively, his lip curled in a sneer. He had a shaved head and wore a karate *gi* tied with a black belt. 'Let's get on with it.'

He shoved open the door and marched in. 'Come on then!' His booming voice echoed back from the ceiling of the *kwoon*. 'Get in here!'

The team hurried after him.

'Form your lines!' boomed the man.

Most of the students scurried to line up in two files. Matt didn't. Where was Chang?

'Who is this guy?' whispered Matt, hanging back.

'No idea,' said Olivier.

'I don't get it,' muttered Catarina.

'Nor do I,' said Shawn. 'Chang didn't say anything –'

'Hey!' roared the man. 'You four – I told you to get in line, and when I give an order I

expect to see some action! Fifty press-ups –
now!'

Matt and the other Tigers hesitated.

'If you don't jump to it, I'll make it a
hundred!'

There didn't seem to be any choice.

'Who does he think he is?' Catarina
whispered to the others. 'Some sort of
sergeant major?'

Matt's lips twitched, but he knew he could
not afford to let a smile escape. The Tangshan
Tigers threw themselves down and started on
the press-ups. Matt felt stiff after yesterday's
work-out, but he gritted his teeth and pushed
against the floorboards, feeling his muscles
strain.

'Right!' said the newcomer, addressing the
whole squad. 'Allow me to introduce myself.
I'm Sensei Mike Ryan.'

Matt heard Carl say 'Cool!' It sounded as
though he'd heard of Ryan.

'You'd probably like to know a bit about me,' went on Ryan loudly. 'So here goes.' He took out a remote-control handset and pressed a button. A flat screen smoothly descended from the ceiling. Matt watched as he continued to press his hands into the floor, raising himself up and down, keeping his back straight and his toes curled beneath his body. A picture of Ryan appeared on the screen. He was standing on a podium with a gold medal.

'I'm a karate black belt, fifth *dan*. Three times world heavyweight karate champion.'

There was a clip of Ryan in competition, putting together a fantastic combination of kicks and punches, knocking his opponent clean off his feet. Then there was a roar of applause from the crowd that had been watching.

'That was when I won the heavyweight championship for the third time,' said Ryan.

'I'm also a second-degree tae kwon-do black belt. Finalist in American championships two years running.' Another clip of Ryan fighting, this time in a tae kwon-do bout. As a practitioner himself, Matt could appreciate the speed and skill with which he fought. He was so transfixed, he almost forgot to continue with his press-ups. He lowered himself to the floor. A drip of sweat fell from the tip of his nose on to the floorboards and his arm muscles were trembling.

'When will this end?' panted Olivier. Matt couldn't even answer him, he was too exhausted.

'I'm also trained in wrestling and ju-jitsu,' Ryan continued. 'And I've coached the karate team at Stanford University.' Another picture, of Ryan standing, arms folded, in the centre of a team of students. 'So you could say I've got quite a CV.' He clicked another button and the screen went blank. 'Any questions?'

Carl's hand shot up. 'What was it like winning the world karate championship three times?'

'Hard work. But it was worth it. And it got better each time.'

'Do you still compete?'

'I pick my competitions more carefully now, but, yeah, I still compete.'

'How did you find time to learn so many different martial arts?' That was from Vincent.

'Dedication.' Matt looked up and saw the smile of self-satisfaction that lit up Ryan's face. *I'm not sure I like this man*, he thought.

'What's the most effective form of martial art?' asked Andrei Drago. Matt had to admit that was a good question. He waited to see how Ryan would respond.

'You need a combination. Knowing any one stand-up form, like karate or tae kwon-do, is good. Knowing two is better – you can keep opponents guessing. But you also need a thorough knowledge of a take-down style, like wrestling or ju-jitsu, if you're to be really dangerous.'

Matt was on press-up twenty-six now. His muscles felt as though they were tearing apart. Even so, he managed to gasp out: 'Did Chang Sifu send you to talk to us?'

'No, he didn't,' said Ryan curtly. 'There's one very obvious question no one's asked yet. Don't you want to know why I'm here?'

'OK,' said Carl taking a step forward. 'Why are you here?'

'Say hello to your new teacher,' said Ryan.

Matt fell face down on the floor. What was this show-off doing, saying he was their teacher? Had Chang Sifu abandoned them, after all? Ryan glared at him.

'Get up and finish those press-ups!' he barked. 'Now listen up, everyone. If you all do exactly what I say, we'll get on fine. If not,

33

look out for trouble. I'm going to work you hard, harder than you've ever been worked before. Because that's what you need.'

There was a moment's pause. Ryan stood, hands on hips, sizing up the group. He walked over to the Tangshan Tigers, who were struggling with the last few press-ups.

'Pathetic!' boomed Ryan. 'You're not in shape; you're a disgrace! I can do fifty press-ups one-handed without breaking sweat! Now, get up, you four, and join the lines.'

'Excuse me, sir,' ventured Matt. He was desperate to know what had happened to Chang. 'What about Chang Sifu?'

Ryan stared at Matt without speaking for a moment. Then he said: 'Don't worry about Chang. He's history.'

The Tangshan Tigers looked at each other in dismay. Matt saw Catarina compress her lips.

'As I understand it,' said Ryan, 'you managed to win your last tournament, but only just. It

34

could have gone the other way. You shouldn't
be scraping through tournaments like that,
you should be trampling all over the
opposition! I aim to toughen you lot
up – so let's get started. Jogging on the spot
now!'

The students started to jog at once.

'Faster! Get those knees up, get them right
up!'

The jogging went on for five minutes. Matt,
already tired from the press-ups, felt ready to
drop. He saw Shawn gasping for breath,
Catarina's head drooping, Olivier jogging
slower and slower. Lola was groaning aloud.

'And now,' shouted Ryan, 'squat thrusts!
Like this!'

He dropped to his hands and began
pumping his legs violently backwards and
forwards between his arms.

The students also dropped to their hands.
Matt's biceps screamed in protest. Everyone

began moving their legs back and forth slowly.

'Faster!' roared Ryan. 'You can do better than that!'

The squat thrusts went on for another five minutes.

'Now sit-ups!' shouted Ryan. He swivelled on to his back, stretched his legs out, put his hands behind his head, and started doing sit-ups, bending forward fast and furiously so his head bobbed against his knees. 'Like this! Fifty of them! Hands behind heads – anyone uses their arms to cheat, it's fifty press-ups for the whole squad!'

Somehow Matt got through his sit-ups. But as he lowered his back for the final time, he felt a muscle in his stomach burn with pain. Matt collapsed to the floor. One by one, the rest of the squad slumped to the floor, groaning, trying to recover their breath. Matt's stomach muscles ached badly and something had definitely pulled. He stretched his arms above his head and winced. He'd never enjoyed a training session less.

He was prepared to work his heart out for Chang, but Ryan seemed nothing more than a bully. The session felt more like a punishment than training.

'All right, stop panting like that,' said Ryan. He had barely broken sweat. 'You're not fit, you lot, that's your trouble.'

He scanned the breathless students in front of him. 'There are twelve of you. But there should be eleven in the squad. Who's the odd man out?'

'It's Andrei Drago, Sensei,' said Carl. Matt could tell he was impressed by Sensei Ryan. 'Andrei's just joined us from another school, and Ch– our old instructor said he could train with us.' Carl didn't even want to say Chang's name any more, Matt noted bitterly.

Ryan addressed Drago. 'I've heard about you.'

'Oh?' Drago looked uneasy, biting his lip.

37

Maybe he was wondering if Ryan knew about his activities in Kyoto.

'Yeah. Desperate to get in the team, aren't you? I like your style. I want people who are determined to win in my team!'

What? thought Matt. *So nearly poisoning people with sleeping gas is some sort of recommendation?*

Drago looked proud of himself. 'I'm determined, Sensei. I'll do whatever it takes.'

Ryan nodded. 'That's good. Now, we're going to work on power today – and we'll use this power drill as a new try-out. In my view, it's good to have try-outs regularly. Keeps you on your toes, stops you taking your place for granted.'

Ryan went over to the equipment room and threw the door open. 'Got some padded body protectors in here. Everybody grab one – you're going to need it.'

As he buckled on his body protector, Matt's

thoughts went back to Chang again. How could this have happened? And why? His feeling yesterday that something wasn't right had been spot on, after all.

Shawn grimaced at him.

'We've got to find out where Chang's gone!' said Matt.

'I know,' said Shawn. 'But how?'

'Right, everybody pair off and find a space on the mat!' boomed Ryan. 'You and you together, you and you, yes, and you two . . .'

Matt found himself paired with Carl.

'Hey, I bet you don't feel so special now you're not the coach's pet!' sneered Carl.

'Don't talk to me,' said Matt. 'Let's just do the drill.'

'Stand one arm's length apart!' said Ryan. 'Using the style you're used to, the drill is to strike your opponent in the target area of the body as many times as you can and as hard as you can. Obviously you may block your

39

opponent's attacks, but what I'm looking for here is aggression. And power. The harder you hit, the more chance you have of keeping your place in the squad! Right, let's go!'

Without any warning, Carl landed a thumping strike on Matt's chest. Even through the padded body protector Matt felt the force of it.

Carl grinned. 'Pretty good, aren't I?'

Soon the *kwoon* echoed to the sound of fists and feet smacking against body protectors.

Matt knew right away that he wasn't concentrating. Chang had always taught them the importance of focusing. But he couldn't focus – his mind was racing with the reasons why Chang might have disappeared. Was he in danger? And he was also tired from the extra fifty press-ups he'd done and Carl hadn't. At first, he responded well to Carl's attacks, striking back and getting a couple of his trademark tae kwon-do high kicks in. But as the fight continued, he felt his torn stomach muscle getting tighter and tighter. That burning pain had started again and Matt struggled to hold himself upright. He was injured, there was no doubt about it. And as he brought his arm up in a block, he felt a stitch pull at his side. *No!* Matt thought. He couldn't have an injury now; Ryan would just accuse him of being weak. And more importantly he had a mystery to investigate.

Carl, on the other hand, was injury-free and showing off to the new coach. Carl got in three blows to every two of Matt's – and he hit hard too. Matt had never absorbed the full force of his strikes before, and he had to admit he was impressed by his power. Carl might be boastful, but he did know how to fight.

'OK!' shouted Ryan. 'And relax!'

The smack of fists and feet died away. The only sound was students breathing hard. Many were bent double, or stood with their hands on their knees, trying to get their breath back.

'Stand up straight!' ordered Ryan.

He walked around the *kwoon*, staring into the face of each student. When he came to Andrei, Matt saw their eyes meet and a look of understanding seemed to pass between them. Was that a sly smile on Andrei's lips? He seemed to be enjoying this training! Ryan gave an almost imperceptible nod and moved on.

He paused in front of Matt. His cold eyes bored into him. Matt felt an eyelid twitch as he forced himself not to drop his gaze. He wouldn't give in, wouldn't be psyched out!

'You seemed to be struggling, Matt,' Ryan said. 'Is everything OK with your fitness?'

'Fine, sir. Never better,' Matt replied, pulling his shoulders straight. No way was he going to admit to Ryan that the sit-ups had hurt him.

At last, Ryan grunted and moved away. He returned to the front and addressed the whole group. 'I have made my decision,' he said. There was an agonizing pause. 'You've all trained well today. Every one of you has shown skill and commitment and plenty of hard work – so, well done for that. I've decided that young Andrei is worthy of a place on the team.'

'Yes!' said Drago, punching the air.

Ryan looked at him sternly. Drago dropped his hands to his sides and composed himself. But he couldn't stop the smile that played on his lips.

I knew it, thought Matt. The way they'd looked at each other, the way Ryan had nodded . . . *It's a set-up!*

'It's unfortunate that someone has to go to make room for him,' said Ryan. 'The student who will be dropped is . . .'

His eyes roved around the room, alighting briefly on each student in turn. Finally it came to rest on . . .

'Matt,' said Sensei Ryan.

Matt felt as if he had taken a punch in the

gut – harder than any of Carl's blows. He could hear the rush of blood in his ears. He heard Catarina gasp in dismay, Shawn saying 'What?' and Olivier crying 'No!' Surely this was a bad dream?

But it wasn't a dream. The sarcastic slap on the back Carl gave him felt all too real.

'Bad luck, mate!' said Carl. 'Still, maybe you could take up another sport? Maybe there's a place on the girls' netball team!'

'Shut up, Carl,' said Catarina.

'Oh well, if he can't take a joke . . .' sneered Carl. He turned away and went to congratulate Drago. 'Congratulations, mate! High five!'

Drago grinned. 'High five!'

'Training session over!' said Sensei Ryan. 'Go and get changed and go to your lessons.'

The squad began to pile into the changing rooms, exclaiming loudly about the events of the session. Drago and Carl were laughing together.

Matt ran out of the door into the corridor. He didn't want to speak to anyone, didn't want to be with people he couldn't call teammates any more.

He came to a halt in front of a big landscape window that looked out over the bustling city of Beijing. Was Chang out there somewhere? Had he already left the school?

The Tangshan Tigers ran out after him and clustered round, trying to console him.

'Hey, that wasn't fair!' said Olivier. 'You're one of the best, we all know that!'

'But I wasn't at my best today,' said Matt, massaging his stomach. 'I was thinking about Chang.'

'Well, if this guy's here to stay and he's holding regular try-outs, you're bound to get back in the squad,' said Shawn.

'Yeah. Well. Maybe,' said Matt.

He did his best to put his disappointment to one side. There was no point wallowing in it.

45

'Let's not worry about it now. There's something more important to worry about.' Matt swivelled round to face his friends. 'Where's Chang?'

INVESTIGATING SENSEI

'We could go and look in Chang's office,' said Shawn. 'We'll be late for class, but –'

'Don't worry about that,' said Olivier. 'I'll think of a story to keep Mrs Barraclough happy.'

'Let's go!' said Matt.

They sprinted down the corridor. At the junction with another corridor they skidded to a sudden stop as Miss Lee, the Principal's secretary, almost walked into them. She was a severe woman with her hair scraped back into a bun. She looked at the Tangshan Tigers disapprovingly.

47

'Why are you not in class? The bell went –' she consulted her wristwatch – 'four and a half minutes ago.'

'We're on an errand for Sensei Ryan,' said Olivier smoothly. 'Delivering a message.'

'I see. Well, please remember that it is forbidden to run in corridors.'

'Sorry, Miss Lee!'

They walked on quietly until Miss Lee was out of sight, then, without a word, broke into a sprint all at the same time.

There was the door with Chang's name in gold letters in both the Roman alphabet and Chinese characters. Matt tapped at it.

No answer.

He turned the handle – the last time Chang had unexpectedly disappeared, the Tigers had found a clue to his whereabouts in his office. The door swung open to reveal a bare room containing nothing but a desk and chair.

Chang's books had gone. So had his painting of a tiger. The Tigers looked under the desk and chair and on the window sill behind the blinds, and Matt even turned up a corner of the carpet. But there was not a hint of Chang: no scrap of paper, no hidden message, nothing to give them a lead.

'What now?' said Catarina.

'I think we should go and see Mr Wu,' said Olivier. 'I mean, he is the Principal, he ought to know what's going on!'

They hurried to Mr Wu's office, arriving just as the bell for morning break was ringing. At least they didn't need to think of an excuse for not being in class. Matt knocked at the door.

'Yes?' said Mr Wu. He stood in the doorway, immaculate as always in his well-cut suit, glittering steel spectacles and neatly trimmed moustache. He was holding the basketball trophy that Matt's room-mate Johnny had won with his team last season in one hand and a

49

feather duster in the other. 'Can I help you?'

'We were wondering,' said Olivier in his most winning manner, 'if you could tell us anything about where Master Chang has gone. If he's left, you see, we'd like to say goodbye, get him a present –'

'I'm afraid that is unlikely to be possible. I will pass on your good wishes if I speak to him again.' He flicked a final speck of dust from the basketball trophy. All around the room, gleaming trophies stood on shelves. Mr Wu picked up another – Soccer, 2005 – and began dusting that one.

'So he has definitely left? For good?'

'Really, the staffing of this Academy is not something students need concern themselves with,' said Mr Wu. *He seems flustered*, Matt thought. He couldn't look any of the Tangshan Tigers in the eye. He picked up a swimming cup. 'The fact is that I – and the governors – reached a decision that it was no longer in the best interests of the school for Master Chang to continue as martial arts coach.'

'But he helped us win the last two tournaments!' said Matt.

'Er, yes, but at this point it was felt . . .' Mr Wu allowed the sentence to tail away. 'Sensei Ryan also has an excellent record as a coach.'

'But I don't understand!' Catarina burst out. 'You sacked Chang? Why? What did he do?'

There was a tap at the connecting door and Miss Lee came in from her adjoining room. 'Is everything all right? I heard loud voices.' She gave the Tangshan Tigers a bemused look.

'Everything is under control, Miss Lee,' said Mr Wu, waving his feather duster at her. 'There is no need to fuss. Please leave us.'

The door closed behind Miss Lee. Mr Wu coughed and continued, 'Er, this is not a matter that children would understand. Better not to worry your heads over it. I can tell you, however, that Chang was not sacked. It was felt he was no longer the best choice as coach. We offered him an alternative position as professor of Chinese history, a subject in which he has considerable depth of knowledge – but he declined.' Mr Wu put down his duster and spread his hands in a gesture of innocence. 'What more could I do?'

'So where is Chang now?' asked Shawn.

The Principal moved past the Tigers to get to another shelf of trophies. He started flicking his handkerchief at a gymnastics trophy. 'I am not Master Chang's keeper. Now he has left the Academy I have no responsibility for him. He is – wherever he has gone. Now if you will excuse me, I have much work to be getting on with.'

He pushed past Matt and started dusting another trophy – and this one, Matt saw with a pang, was the replica jade dish that Chang had helped them win in their first tournament together.

'But —' began Catarina loudly. Matt saw she was on the point of flaring up, and he knew exactly how she felt. But what good would it do to get into a row with Mr Wu? He gently tugged Catarina's arm.

'Let's go,' he said quietly.

The Tangshan Tigers walked away. Matt heard Mr Wu close his office door firmly behind them.

'Something's not right here!' said Catarina, smacking her fist into her palm.

'I agree,' said Matt. 'But we'd better not discuss it here in the corridor. We might be overheard.'

'Does that matter?' said Olivier.

'It might,' said Matt, glancing over his shoulder. 'This looks like a case for the Tangshan Tigers. Come on, let's go to the Walled Garden.'

The Walled Garden was a paved, enclosed space behind the Common Room, a secluded spot that was a good place for secret discussions. It had wooden benches and a cherry tree, as well as a fountain that sprang from a little pile of rocks, lit from below with a constantly changing light that made the water glow green, then blue, then red, then amber in turn.

'Catarina's right that something's up,' said Matt. 'Chang did say that he wouldn't leave us willingly. I just don't believe that Chang would go without saying goodbye.'

'No,' said Shawn. 'No way.'

'Whatever made him leave either happened very suddenly, or behind his back. Either way, it looks suspicious,' Olivier said.

'Well, we've got to investigate it then,' said Matt. 'And put it right!'

'But how are we going to do that?' said Olivier. 'Nearly all our time outside of class is going to be taken up with training –'

'And recovering from training, if this

morning's session was anything to go by,' added Shawn.

'You guys won't have much spare time,' said Matt. 'But I will. I'm not in the squad any more, am I?'

The other Tigers looked uneasy, Matt saw. They weren't comfortable about having their friend shoved off the team.

'Maybe we should all quit,' said Catarina. 'Tell Ryan if he doesn't want you he can't have us either!'

'There's no need for that,' said Matt. 'I don't want the whole squad to break up just because of me. I can get on with investigating on my own.'

He walked over to the lift to go to his dorm.

The Tigers followed him.

'But – we're a team, right?' said Shawn. 'I mean, we're supposed to work together –'

'I'll keep you posted on whatever I find out,'

said Matt. He pressed the lift button. 'Don't worry, we're in this together. But it makes sense for me to get on with it – I'm the one with time on my hands!'

'What are you going to do?' asked Olivier.

'I'm thinking about who benefits from Chang leaving,' said Matt. 'It's Sensei Ryan, right? He's got a new job out of it. I'm going to find out all I can about the man, see if he could be behind it in any way.'

'Sounds like a good idea,' said Shawn.

'Well, I'll let you know,' said Matt.

The lift doors silently opened. Matt stepped in.

'Good luck!' said Olivier.

'Sure thing,' said Matt.

The lift doors closed. The high-speed elevator whisked him up to the dorm. *I'll find out what's happened*, thought Matt. *I have to.*

Matt made his way to the room he shared with Johnny Goldberg. Johnny wasn't there –

he was off training with the basketball team. *Everyone's training, except me*, thought Matt, but he pushed the thought away. It was time to get on with his task.

He sat down at the computer on the desk under the window and got on to the Internet. He tapped in 'Sensei Mike Ryan' and hit Search.

A few seconds' pause, and the flat screen filled up with hits for Mike Ryan. The first screen of fifty. Over five hundred hits. The man had an international reputation, there was no disputing that.

Matt began to work through the links, starting with Ryan's official website. A picture of Ryan's unsmiling face appeared, chin tilted upwards aggressively. Matt jumped as a booming voice filled the room.

'Hi, I'm Mike Ryan. Three times heavyweight karate champion. Twice winner of the Philippines open championship. Member of the American Olympic karate team for the Athens Olympics. Tae kwon-do black belt . . .'

The list went on and on. There was a host of tournaments, in both karate and tae kwon-do, that Ryan had won, and he'd even won a number of extreme cage fighting competitions. His record was pretty much on the same level as that of Chang. Matt found himself wondering who would have won if they'd fought each other when both were in their prime. *Surely Chang would know too much for Ryan*, Matt thought loyally. But there was no way of really being sure.

He quit the official website and explored some of the other hits. Sensei Ryan was senior instructor of a karate federation, Matt discovered, with schools all over the world. It was more of an honorary than an active position now, but according to the website he had set up the federation himself some years ago. That looked interesting.

Matt clicked on the link for the federation website. This was getting even more interesting. He went from link to link, finding out more and more. Nearly an hour had gone by when he finally straightened up, drew a deep breath and shut down the computer.

Hope you find out a few things, Olivier had said.

Well, he'd done that all right.

Matt raced downstairs and reached the *kwoon* just as the Tangshan Tigers were leaving after training – except it wasn't called the *kwoon* any more, Matt noticed. Sensei Ryan had replaced the sign with one saying *dojo*, the Japanese term used by *karateka*. It was as though every trace of Chang was being removed.

'Well? Did you turn up anything?' asked Olivier.

'You could say that,' said Matt, deliberately casual.

'What?'

59

'Let's just get away from here – don't want anyone to overhear.'

He led the way down the passage to a quiet stairwell.

'Tell us!' said Shawn. 'Don't keep us in suspense!'

'Ryan's senior instructor of a federation of karate schools.'

'The Ryan Karate Federation,' said Olivier. 'I think I've heard of it.'

'Yes, it's a pretty big business,' said Matt. 'International. Must be worth a lot of money. He started it himself about ten years ago. But how did he get the money to set it up?'

'Don't know,' said Catarina impatiently. 'How?'

A school security guard wandered past, whistling off-key, and the Tangshan Tigers ducked further into the shadows. Matt waited for the guard to disappear round a corner.

'A friend from his university days lent him

the money,' he continued. 'He'd done well for himself, this friend – he was a famous scientist and he'd patented some inventions.'

'And?' said Catarina. 'What about this friend?'

'What's his name?' asked Olivier.

'Oh, didn't I mention his name?' said Matt. 'It's Vitali Drago.'

The Tigers stared at Matt.

'You mean – Andrei's father?' said Shawn.

'That's right,' said Matt. 'Andrei's father.'

'So that's it!' said Olivier. 'Mr Wu said it wasn't in the best interests of the school for Chang to continue here –'

'The best interests of the school would be to receive a whole lot of money from Old Man Drago, on condition his son gets in the martial arts squad!' said Catarina.

'And Andrei's not good enough to be sure of a place with Chang as coach – and there's no way you could bribe Chang!' said Shawn.

'But Ryan – of course he'll put Andrei in the squad. He owes his dad, big-time!' finished Olivier.

'Yes,' said Matt. 'It's the only explanation that makes sense. We know that Andrei's dad can pull strings – it must have been him who got his son off the hook in Kyoto. Now he's at it again!'

'The question is, what do we do now?' said Olivier. 'Not much use going to Mr Wu about it.'

'Obviously not,' said Matt. 'But we really need someone we can tell, an adult we can trust . . .'

'Master Chang!' said Catarina.

'Right,' said Matt. 'If we tell him what's been happening, he'll be able to think of something. He always does.'

'Yeah, but how do we find him?' said Olivier. 'No one knows where he's gone. Last time, at least he left a clue, but this time –'

'This time there's nothing,' said Matt heavily.

Unexpectedly, Shawn grinned. 'Nothing visible, anyway.'

'What do you mean?' demanded Catarina.

'You'll see,' said Shawn. 'Meet me at Chang's office!'

'But what . . .?'

Shawn didn't stay to answer. He was already running down the corridor.

FOLLOWING SIFU'S TRAIL

Matt, Catarina and Olivier were waiting at Chang's door when Shawn turned up a few minutes later, out of breath. He was carrying a strange black machine, a metal box on wheels with a sort of robot head sticking out. He set it down on the floor in front of his friends with an air of pride.

'Here we are!' he said.

'Er, Shawn,' said Matt. 'What is it?'

'It's an Electro-Hound,' said Shawn.

'A what?'

My dad sent it to me. It's the prototype of a

new toy; gonna be the next big thing in the States. It's kind of a robot dog, see? It's programmed to recognize certain scents – you can send it to fetch chocolate, or cookies, or whatever. Pretty neat, huh?'

'Yes, and it would be really handy if we needed to find some chocolate or cookies right now,' said Olivier. 'However, since we're trying to find a missing martial arts master, it may not be quite –'

'But the point is, I've modified it a little bit!' said Shawn. 'I was just tinkering around, and I've managed to re-programme it to learn new scents.'

Matt and the others couldn't help laughing. How on earth did Shawn find time to do all this?

'You mean – it'll find Chang's scent?' asked Matt.

'That's the idea!' said Shawn. 'Watch!'

He pressed a button on the remote-control

handset. The Electro-Hound emitted a whirring noise. Its eyes glowed red. It scooted into Chang's office, making an electronic sniffing, snuffling sound.

'Oh, it's so cute!' said Catarina.

Shawn sent the Electro-Hound all over Chang's office, sniffing out the areas where he would have spent most time: his chair, the window, the small Buddhist shrine where Chang meditated.

The snuffling noise suddenly stopped. It was replaced by an excited bleeping. The Electro-Hound's stumpy tail began waving madly.

'It's done it!' said Shawn. 'It's picked up the scent!'

'Amazing!' said Matt. 'And now – we follow it, do we?'

'Sure,' said Shawn. 'Just like a real tracking dog.'

'Problem,' said Olivier. 'Afternoon school's about to begin. Maybe we should wait –'

'No,' said Matt firmly. 'Let's not waste any time – the sooner we find Chang, the better.'

'How are we going to get out of school without being spotted, though?' asked Catarina. 'There're security guards at all the doors!'

Olivier clicked his fingers. 'I have an idea. Wait here – I'm going to get something from my room.'

He hurried out. The Tigers shared a puzzled glance.

The Electro-Hound was still bleeping. 'I'd better shut this thing up,' said Shawn. 'They might think it's a bit strange if we walk out with it bleeping away.' He picked it up. 'Be quiet, Hound!'

The bleeping stopped. 'You mean – it does what you say?' marvelled Catarina.

'Actually, I just switched it off!' grinned Shawn. He tucked the Hound under his jacket.

Olivier returned, holding four plastic ring binders. 'Here you are.'

Matt took his and opened it. It was full of blank sheets of paper.

'What's this?'

'You'll find out,' said Olivier. 'Let's go!'

The Tigers followed Olivier to one of the side-exits of the school. A young, fresh-faced security guard was on duty there. His uniform was pressed and spotless, his cap-badge gleaming. He looked up questioningly as the Tigers approached, their official-looking folders tucked under their arms.

'Yes?'

'Could you let us through, please?' said Olivier in an English accent. 'We're in rather a hurry.'

Matt looked at him in surprise – Olivier had a gift for doing different accents but Matt hadn't heard this one before. It was spot on, the type of clipped British accent that carried irresistible authority.

'May I see your pass, please?' asked the guard respectfully.

'We have an appointment to meet with students from a local school for the new Outreach Programme – you know all about that, I suppose?'

'Er – Outreach Programme?'

'You mean they haven't briefed you?' said Olivier in a tone of incredulity. 'Really, I did think this would have been better organized. The new Outreach Programme is an initiative for Beijing International Academy students to help the education of local primary-school children – teaching them English, you know. I'd have thought Mr Wu would have told all the staff about it – but you're fairly new to the job, aren't you? Perhaps the briefing was before you joined?'

'Er – perhaps, but –'

'Well, you can always check with Mr Wu

later. But right now we are in rather a rush, so if you wouldn't mind . . .'

The guard still looked undecided. 'Why are you leaving by the side entrance?'

'It's quicker,' said Olivier. 'And as I said we are in something of a rush. You wouldn't want to be responsible for BIA not honouring its commitments, would you? I don't know what Mr Wu would say about that!'

The other Tigers, standing behind Olivier, joined in the act. Matt looked at his watch; Shawn impatiently riffled through the pages in his ring binder; Catarina loudly muttered, 'I dunno what the Embassy will say if we're late, they're not gonna like it . . .'

'All right,' said the guard finally. 'Outreach Programme – yes, I think I did hear something about it. Go on then.' He waved them through the door.

They left the building, walking quickly. They

came out into a quiet side street, lined with trees.

'Made it!' said Olivier.

'Mm,' said Matt. 'I just wish, sometimes, we didn't have to tell such huge lies.'

'Hey, the end justifies the means; that's what my dad says!' said Olivier.

'What does that mean?' asked Catarina.

'It means it's OK to bend the rules a bit if it's in a good cause,' said Olivier. 'Besides, that Outreach programme seems like a pretty good idea to me – I might suggest it to Mr Wu. So it won't really be a lie – just the truth a little bit in advance!'

Shawn put the Electro-Hound down and switched it on. Immediately it began bleeping and scooted off down the road.

The Tangshan Tigers hurried after it. The Hound took them down a street of apartments with a scattering of shops, and a cafe with a red and white Coca-Cola umbrella, where barefoot old men played chess.

71

'So Chang must have come this way?' asked Matt.

'That's right,' said Shawn.

'But hold on,' said Matt. He thought he'd spotted a flaw in the plan. 'What if Chang didn't walk all the way to wherever he was going? I mean, he might have got a bus or a taxi at some point. Won't the Hound lose the scent?'

'That's the clever bit,' Shawn answered. 'The Hound can always lead us to the last place a scent was located. From there, he should be able to pick up airborne scents and there's a chance we can locate the next place Chang went to. I can't promise, but it might just work. We might be able to track Chang to anywhere in this city!'

They had reached a main road. Cars, buses and lorries thundered past. The Electro-Hound came to a halt. It stopped bleeping. Its eyes flashed red.

'What's it doing?'

'This must be where the trail goes cold,' said Shawn. 'Wait.'

There was a tinkling – the sound Shawn's BlackBerry made when a new email arrived. He took it from his pocket and showed the Tigers the colour display on the screen. Matt saw a map of Beijing and its environs. A red dot was flashing on and off.

'That's Chang!' said Shawn. 'Or that's the nearest point the Hound can pick up the scent. He might have moved on from there by now, but we'll get a better reading when we're closer.'

'We need take on the third ring road around the city,' said Olivier. 'But it's too far to walk all the way – how are we going to get there?'

'Let's get started, anyway,' said Catarina.

They walked along the pavement to a junction where the road split into three. Several passers-by paused to stare at the robot dog, rumbling along by their side.

'That's the third ring road!' said Catarina, pointing. 'We gotta cross the first two!'

Using pedestrian crossings, they made their way over to the third ring road.

'And here comes our lift!' said Catarina.

She pointed at a truck with an open trailer. The driver wore an old blue cap and a dirty yellow vest; a cigarette hung from his lips. The truck was heading their way, rattling along. The driver blared his horn as he swerved, without touching the brakes, to avoid a cyclist whizzing past him.

Matt felt the blood drain from his face. 'You're joking, aren't you?'

'What's the joke?' said Catarina. 'We jump in the back. No problem.'

'But it's far too dangerous!'

Catarina raised her eyebrows. 'I never expected to hear that from a Tangshan Tiger! You gonna quit without even trying?'

Matt felt stung. 'I'm not a quitter!' he said. 'Just watch me!'

'No, you better watch me!' said Catarina. 'I'll show you how to do it.'

Staying low, she led the way as the Tangshan Tigers ran along beside the truck. Shawn snatched up the Electro-Hound and stuffed it inside his jacket. The truck pulled ahead, but it slowed down to take the bend as the ring road peeled off to the right. For a few precious seconds they were catching up.

'Now's the moment!' said Catarina. Sprinting at top speed, she reached out and put a hand on the tailgate of the trailer. In one graceful movement, she vaulted into the trailer, her long legs arcing through the air.

Shawn and Olivier followed, not quite as gracefully as Catarina, but efficiently enough.

Now it was Matt's turn. He was breathless and his heart was hammering like a machine gun. The Tigers were beckoning to him, holding out their hands.

'Come on, Matt!' called Olivier. 'Nearly there!'

Matt was running as fast as he could, but already the truck was picking up speed. He reached out, but could not quite close the gap of a metre or so between him and the trailer. If he didn't jump soon he'd be left behind!

'Come on, Matt!' shouted Catarina. 'You can do it!'

Matt put on a desperate spurt, grabbed for the tailgate, and jumped. His legs were swept off the ground. For a moment he dangled perilously, the road rushing by beneath him. The muscle in his stomach was really pulling, but Matt couldn't let go now. The truck swayed, shaking him from side to side. He heard horns blaring, and knew that if he fell it would be right in the path of the traffic behind.

Then he felt the hands of Catarina, Shawn

and Olivier grabbing his arms, holding him tight, hauling him in.

He tumbled into the back of the trailer, gasping for breath.

He'd made it!

The trailer was filled with sacks of wheat. The Tangshan Tigers sat up and grinned at each other. In the cabin of the truck, the driver was listening to loud music from the radio, nodding his head, tapping with his hand on the steering wheel. He had no idea he was carrying four passengers.

The Tangshan Tigers exchanged triumphant high fives.

'See?' said Catarina. 'I told you there was no problem!'

'Right,' laughed Matt. 'No problem at all.'

Just at that moment, the Hound began to bleep again.

'Why's it doing that?' asked Matt.

'We're going off course,' said Shawn,

77

consulting his BlackBerry. 'Getting further away from Chang. We better get off as soon as we can.'

He sat up and peered over the rim of the trailer.

'We're just coming up to the Suzhou Bridge. There are two streams of traffic that join together just before the bridge, so the truck will have to slow down – that's when we get off.'

Matt felt the truck begin to decelerate.

'Here goes!' said Catarina. With one hand she vaulted lightly over the side. This time Matt didn't have the slightest hesitation in following her. His confidence was high and he knew he could do it. He jumped out nimbly and hit the ground running – he felt almost as light and agile as Catarina herself. The other two also jumped out. The driver cast a surprised look out of the window as four kids suddenly appeared out of nowhere, running along the pavement beside his truck.

Matt bowed and said '*Xie yi*,' the Mandarin phrase for 'Thank you'.

The driver, still looking bemused, nodded before speeding away. Laughing, the Tangshan Tigers slowed to a walk.

'Which way now?' said Olivier.

'Let's ask the Hound,' said Shawn. He placed it on the ground and it began bleeping again. It added an excited, electronic bark. 'This way!' Shawn cried.

The Hound led them along the pavement for a while and then they turned off the main road. They followed a winding, tree-lined track uphill. The sounds of the traffic grew remote.

The Hound raced along, its bleeping getting faster. Presently the Tangshan Tigers found themselves standing on a grassy hill, overlooking a broad, shimmering green lake. Between them and the lake was a high wire fence. On the opposite side of the lake, surrounded by trees, was a white building.

'This must be Longevity Hill and that must be Kunming Lake,' said Shawn, checking the map on his BlackBerry. 'It's in the grounds of the Summer Palace.'

Matt gazed over the grounds of the palace. Somewhere in there was Chang. The man-made lake and its surroundings were beautiful. A spectacular bridge crossed the lake at its midpoint, its graceful arches reflected in the water so that they seemed to form perfect circles. Matt counted the arches – there were seventeen.

He breathed deeply. 'You could only see something like this in Beijing,' he said. 'Amazing.'

'Yes,' said a familiar voice. 'Sometimes nature and art can join together, to create something more beautiful than either alone.'

Matt spun round. Chang Sifu stepped out from a clump of trees. The Electro-Hound raced up to him and sniffed the hems of his trousers, his shiny black metal tail wagging furiously back and forth.

Chang smiled down at the Electro-Hound. 'You found me then,' he said.

EXPLANATION

'Sifu!' said Matt.

He made the traditional sign of respect, placing his right fist into his open left hand. The other Tigers did the same. Chang acknowledged the gesture with a slight movement of the head. He did not seem surprised to see the Tangshan Tigers, but then Chang seldom appeared to be surprised by anything.

But what was he doing here? There was no sign of habitation nearby, unless one counted the distant Summer Palace. Surely Chang wasn't sleeping rough? His hair was dishevelled and he looked tired. Then Matt caught sight of a small wooden hut, or shed, some way off behind the trees. Was that where Chang was staying?

'Why did you come here, Sifu?' he asked respectfully. 'Why did you leave the Academy?'

'Circumstances made it necessary,' Chang replied. He began to walk across the grass, head bowed as if in deep thought. The Tangshan Tigers followed.

'What circumstances?' asked Shawn.

'Nothing that need affect you.'

'But it does affect us!' said Catarina. 'We know something bad is gonna happen –'

'Otherwise why did you teach us those street-fighting techniques before you left?' asked Matt.

'You are mistaken. I never taught you street-fighting,' said Chang Sifu. He was leading them over to an enclosed garden, with low hedges.

'You know, the centre line theory!' said Shawn, as they stepped into the paths of the garden.

'That is a discipline to improve technique, nothing more. Real fighting, fighting to hurt –' He shook his head. 'It should always be avoided if possible.'

Chang doesn't want to tell us anything, Matt realized. *How are we going to be able to help?*

Olivier tried a different approach, following their teacher among the paths of the garden. 'Sifu, we have discovered something about the appointment of Sensei Ryan. He's an old friend of Andrei Drago's father, who financed his business. And Ryan has put Andrei in the squad – he dropped Matt to make way for him!'

'I am sorry to hear it, Matt,' said Chang evenly. 'But Ryan is in charge of squad now. It is his decision.'

'But it's not fair! It's corruption, isn't it?' said Olivier.

'There is no place for corruption in selection of team, whether I am there or not. Do not accuse Sensei Ryan, or anyone else, without evidence.'

Chang emerged on the other side of the garden. He stopped and gestured at the way back. 'I suggest you return to Academy. Before you get into trouble. Thank you for coming to see me. It shows loyalty. But there is nothing you can do. Go back to Academy.' His face looked tired and Matt noticed the dark circles beneath his teacher's eyes.

'Is that really what you want us to do?' asked Shawn, taking a step closer to the man who had taught them so much.

'Go back to Academy,' repeated Chang. 'Focus on studies. And on training. Always remember: balance is key to everything.' It sounded as though Chang was saying goodbye forever.

'When will we see you again?' Matt asked.

He felt helpless – was there nothing the Tangshan Tigers could do? They'd come all this way to find their teacher.

Sifu turned and walked away. Then he turned and said over his shoulder: 'Remember – the snake approaches silently, but it can be deadly.'

The Tigers exchanged confused glances. *What does Chang mean by talking about snakes?* Matt wondered.

'Do you mean Drago?' asked Catarina. 'Is he the snake?'

Master Chang turned to face them. 'Go back to Academy,' he told them. His voice held a sternness Matt had never heard before. 'You serve no purpose here.' Matt heard Catarina gasp at Chang's words.

The Tangshan Tigers watched as he walked away. This time, he did not look back.

As he approached the hut, Matt saw that there was someone else there now. A small

figure in a blue tunic-dress, stirring a pot
suspended above an open fire. A familiar figure.
It looked like . . .

'Hey, is that Li-Lian?' said Shawn.

'It is!' said Olivier.

She was too far off for Matt to make out
her face, but he knew Chang's granddaughter
by her straight posture, her dainty physique,
the set of her shoulders. She had helped them
fight against Sang and his gang in their
adventure under the Great Wall of China.

At least Chang has some company, thought
Matt. But why had Chang chosen to exile
himself here anyway, in a wooden hut on a
lonely hillside? It was as though he was
deliberately making himself an outcast.

There was nothing more that they could do
for now. Chang had made it plain he did not
want their help. Matt felt hurt and confused.

'Well,' he said, 'I suppose we'd better do as
he says. Go back to the Academy.'

Without another word, they turned and walked back down the track, the Electro-Hound silently bringing up the rear.

Matt did not know what to do next. But he knew one thing. He wasn't going to give up.

'This isn't over,' he said to his friends as they rejoined the main road. 'No way.'

Matt lay in bed, eyes wide open. Through the window he saw a yellow full moon. He threw back the duvet and quietly climbed out of bed.

I'll practise a few tae kwon-do moves, he decided. *Burn off some of this useless energy*. After all, he would have to keep in training if he was ever to get back in the squad. If he was quiet, he needn't wake Johnny. His room-mate was dead to the world, his arms flung out by his side as he slept on his back.

In the centre of the room, he assumed his side-on fighting stance and went through a sequence of moves: circling an imaginary opponent, throwing a few shadow punches, ending with a head-high axe kick. It didn't feel right. He was going through the motions and he knew it. His mind was too distracted to focus on what he was doing. The muscle in his stomach felt like it was healing, despite the occasional twinge. *Try again*, he told himself.

But the second attempt was even worse. He started off-balance, over-corrected and crashed into Johnny's bed.

'What the –' spluttered Johnny. He sat up, blinking, hair sticking up on end. 'What's going on, Matt? Are you sleepwalking? Having a nightmare?'

'No, I was just – er – practising a few moves,' said Matt, feeling foolish.

'In the middle of the night? What, are you crazy?'

'No, I – I couldn't sleep, and I'm worried, and –'

Johnny reached for his glasses on the bedside

table and put them on. 'You better tell me
about it,' he said.

Matt sat down on the end of Johnny's bed.
'You know I got left out of the team?'

'Yeah. That was bad luck.'

'I never thought that would happen to me.
I mean, I felt I belonged there, you know? I
know it doesn't do any good to moan about it,
but – well, that's just how I feel, and I can't
help it. And then Master Chang suddenly
leaving like that – I don't get it. I trusted him
– we all did.

'We went to see him today,' he continued.
'We thought we might be able to help him
get his job back, but he said there's nothing
we can do. Acted like he'd never see us again.
And I don't know if I'll ever get back in the
team without Chang's help!'

Johnny listened thoughtfully, nodding.

'Yeah, that's pretty rough. You know – there
was one time, back at my old school when I

failed the try-outs for the basketball team. And it shook me up, because I always thought I was pretty good at it, like it was my sport, you know?'

'So how did you get over it?'

'How can you not get over it? It's happened, you got to deal with it because there's no other option. I realized the coach had picked the best team, and I wasn't in it, and the team was bigger than any one player. So I watched the school games and I cheered my team. And meantime I kept practising. And the practice paid off because when I came here I made the team! You see? Everything happens for a reason.'

'Everything?' Matt wasn't convinced.

'Well, I guess random stuff happens sometimes, like when somebody gets struck by lightning, but I'd say ninety-nine per cent of the time things happen for a reason. Maybe being dropped from the team will turn out to be a good thing for you in the end – maybe you'll raise your game. There'll even be a reason for Chang leaving.'

'Yeah,' said Matt. 'But what is the reason?'

'Who knows? Maybe you can find out,' Johnny said, pulling the duvet up around his shoulders.

'That's . . . right,' said Matt. He reached over and punched Johnny affectionately on the arm. 'You're a deep thinker, Johnny.'

'Yeah, right!' said Johnny, laughing.

'I better go back to bed then,' said Matt, rising to his feet.

'No,' said Johnny unexpectedly. 'You practise those moves first. And get them right this time!'

Matt took his stance in the centre of the room again. This time he adopted the open stance Chang had taught him for the centre line, with his toes, knees, hips, elbows and shoulders all pointing in the same direction.

He relaxed. He visualized the imaginary line in front of him, a narrow target band on which all his strength would be concentrated. He shifted his balance so that his weight rested firmly on his back foot.

And then he sprang into action.

He moved forward fast and purposefully: block, block, punch, punch, KICK! It felt good, it felt right. Every blow converged on the centre line. Any opponent standing there would have been blown away.

Johnny whisper-mimicked the roar of a crowd. 'Wow!' he said. 'Way to go, Matt!'

Matt bowed. He felt better now. More focused. He got into bed. But before he fell asleep, he made himself a promise. *I'm going to find out why Chang left*, he thought. *And I'm going to get him back here.*

The next day, Matt endured a geography lesson without his friends – the martial arts team were having an extra-long training session and were missing morning classes. At lunchtime, he sat alone at a table in the refectory, eating stir-fried chicken and rice and trying to work out the next step in his plan to help reinstate Chang.

'Sensei Ryan is so cool!' Matt heard Carl Warrick gloat. Carl had his back to Matt; he was sitting with his friends Miles and Roger. Matt pricked up his ears – he might find out something interesting about Ryan.

'We just had the best session with him,' Carl went on. 'Not everyone could keep up, he works us so hard – a few had to stay behind and do extra exercises as a punishment. But not me!'

Oh no, not you, of course, thought Matt sarcastically. He wished Olivier were here to imitate Carl and make him blush.

'He's tons better than that weirdo Chang – who probably left to go and get psychiatric treatment, if you ask me!' Miles and Roger laughed. Matt carried on listening.

'And you know what?' Carl continued. 'I heard him talking on his mobile after the training session – and guess what he said?'

'Dunno,' said Miles. 'What'd he say?'

'He said he's gonna kick someone's butt right off the big bridge!'

Big bridge? Matt's mind started working busily. Which bridge could Ryan mean?

'I reckon he's gonna get us to run laps over that bridge in the Academy gardens, you know? We've trained on it before. I reckon he's going to make us train real hard and anyone who doesn't keep up's gonna get their butt kicked!' Carl laughed. 'I'll keep up, no problem, but it's gonna be funny to see what happens to some of those others!'

Carl's idea doesn't make sense, thought Matt. The bridge in the gardens wasn't particularly big. But what big bridges were there in

Beijing? There were plenty of road bridges, but Ryan would hardly conduct martial arts training on those . . .

The rest of the Tangshan Tigers piled into the refectory.

'Hey, Matt!'

'How's it going?'

Carl turned round as the Tigers sat at Matt's table. 'Oh, it's you guys. Enjoy your fifty press-ups, did you?'

Miles and Roger sniggered.

'I don't know what you're laughing at,' Catarina told them. 'You two wouldn't get near the squad in a million years.'

'Neither will Matt!' said Carl with a grin. 'Ryan won't ever let him back in.' Carl rose from his seat and stood in front of Matt, throwing a few mock karate chops at his face. Matt didn't flinch. He remembered what Chang had said: 'The simple fish snaps at the bait; but the wily old carp is too wise.' If he kept calm, he might find out more about Ryan's phone conversation from Carl, and that might help him find out why Chang had gone.

'When you heard Ryan talking about the big bridge,' he said, 'did he say anything else? Anything about Chang?'

'Why would Ryan waste his time talking about that has-been?' Carl brought a hand down through the air in a vicious karate chop.

'Chang's not a has-been! Ryan's not a patch on him!' said Olivier. He went to stand up out of his seat, but Matt pressed a restraining hand on to his friend's shoulder.

'Chang's past it!' said Carl. 'Ryan's much better than he ever was. The guy's a real hard man, you can see it in his eyes. You know something? He's gonna have a challenge fight, a real one, not a tournament, against some other martial arts guy.'

This was getting interesting. 'A real fight?' said Matt. 'How do you know?'

'Oh, I – I heard him saying about it,' said Carl. 'On his phone. By chance.' His cheeks flushed. *That's the second thing he's overheard Ryan say*, thought Matt. Obviously he hung on the man's every word. Maybe Matt could find out more from him.

'This fight – who's it with? Did he say?'

'Another martial arts guy, a kung fu expert.'

Kung fu? thought Matt. That was Chang's main discipline – though he was expert in other martial arts too.

'It sounds a bit pathetic to me,' remarked Olivier. 'Fixing up fights on his mobile? How old is he? Thirteen?'

'The point is he's man enough to test himself in a real fight!' said Carl. 'Chang would never do that – he wouldn't have the bottle!'

'He's probably picked someone he knows he can beat,' said Matt, hoping to goad Carl into revealing more. 'Some no-hoper who's not even a black belt –'

'Yeah. Well, you're wrong, 'cause he said the guy's got an international reputation and he does other martial arts apart from kung fu, but Ryan says he knows he's got the beating of him!'

International reputation . . . other martial arts apart from kung fu . . . It could be Chang, Matt thought. An image of Chang the last time he'd seen him came to Matt: standing on the hill, his hair slightly dishevelled, behind him the lake with the big arched bridge . . .

Something clicked in Matt's mind. There was no proof, yet it made sense.

'That's it!' he said, banging his fist on the table. Everyone jumped. 'It must be!'

Catarina looked at him curiously. 'What?'

Matt shook his head. He didn't want to talk about it while Carl and his cronies were present. 'Nothing.'

'Totally insane,' said Carl. He pointed his finger at Matt and then at his temple, circling it. Miles and Roger sniggered again as they finished up their lunch.

Matt kept his temper. 'So – when's Ryan having this fight?' he said casually. 'If he's having it at all!'

'Well, you better believe it, because it's this afternoon – that's what I heard him say! So now you know the kind of guy he is – a real fighter, not like old Chang!' Matt leapt out of his seat and gave a few mock punches and kicks into the air, imitating Ryan. Then he ran out of the refectory with his cronies following.

'I think I know who Ryan's fighting,' said Matt quietly. The Tangshan Tigers turned to stare at him.

'Who?' they asked, crowding round.

'Chang,' Matt said, gazing at each of them in turn.

'What?' said Shawn.

'Get outta here!' said Catarina.

'Chang's a kung fu master – and he knows

other martial arts – and he's got an international reputation –'

'Yeah, but there must be hundreds of people . . .' Shawn began.

'But Carl was talking about a big bridge before you came in. That must be the bridge over Kunming Lake – the seventeen-arch one – near where Chang is living!'

'So you think Ryan's challenged Chang? To fight on that bridge in the palace grounds?'

'That's what he's planning, I'm sure of it! It just fits.' Matt got to his feet and walked over to one of the huge windows, looking out over Beijing. In the far distance, he could just see the palace grounds. Was there going to be a fight there? If so, the Tangshan Tigers had to be there for Chang Sifu. They wouldn't let him face this alone.

'But Chang wouldn't do a stupid thing like that!' Shawn called over. 'Like I said, he's a martial artist, not some street brawler!'

Matt swivelled round from the window. 'Maybe Chang doesn't know about it yet! Maybe Ryan's going to attack him and then Chang will have no choice but to fight!'

'Say you're right,' said Catarina. 'What do we do?'

'We have to warn Chang right away. If it's this afternoon, and he doesn't know Ryan's coming for him . . .'

'We have to go back to –' said Shawn.

'Longevity Hill,' interrupted Matt, leaping to his feet. 'And we better go right now!'

SIFU VERSUS SENSEI

The wind blew fiercely on Longevity Hill. A storm was building: black clouds hung low, emitting ominous rumbles of thunder. A driving rain fell.

The Tangshan Tigers ran across the wet grass to Chang's hut.

It was empty. The door was ajar, as if Chang had left in a hurry. Through it, Matt glimpsed the neat, bare interior – two beds, a table, two chairs. In front of the hut were the cold grey ashes of an extinct cooking fire. No Chang, no Li-Lian.

'Maybe they've just gone out – to the shops or something,' suggested Olivier.

'Or maybe they're around somewhere,' said Catarina. 'Let's see if we can get a better view.'

She ran towards the hut and launched herself at the roof. She grabbed the overhanging eave and swung her long legs up. A moment later, she was standing on the roof.

'Hey, nice move, Catarina!' said Matt. 'Can you see anything?'

Catarina scanned the hillside. 'Yes, there are people on the bridge!'

There, at either end of the seventeen-arch bridge, stood two figures. One was dressed in black, the other in white. The figure in black had a shaven head; the figure in white had black hair. With a thud of the heart, Matt realized who he was looking at.

'It's Chang and Ryan!' said Shawn.

As they watched, the figures began to walk towards one another with slow, measured strides.

'Quick! We've got to get down there!' said Matt.

'Do you mean – to stop the fight?' said Olivier. 'But if Chang's agreed to it –'

'Maybe we can talk them out of it,' said Matt. 'Or at least make sure there's fair play. The Dragos are behind this, I'm sure of it!'

'Why them?' asked Olivier.

'Who else? Who was behind Ryan's appointment in the first place? I don't know what they've got against Chang, but getting him turned out of his job wasn't enough for them. Who knows what dirty tricks they'll come up with!'

'OK!' said Catarina. She jumped as lightly as a cat to the ground. 'Let's get down to the bridge and see what we can do.'

She set off at a run over the soggy hillside towards the Summer Palace entrance. The rest of the Tigers followed, catching up just as she arrived at the gates.

Here they were stopped by a guard in military uniform. He was a small man with a peaked cap and a straggly moustache. He held his hand up, palm out, as if he were stopping traffic.

'Sorry, palace grounds closed to visitors now,' he said.

Matt felt desperate. They had to get there before the fight began!

'But there are people down there on the bridge,' he said. 'We saw them.'

'No admittance after four o'clock,' said the guard with satisfaction. 'Grounds close at five.'

'Can't we just come in till five then? We don't want to stay long.'

The guard pushed back his cuff with a flourish and inspected his watch. 'Five past four. No admittance after four o'clock.'

The Tangshan Tigers looked at each other in despair. Even now Chang and Ryan might be beginning their fight – they had to get there before it was too late!

Suddenly Catarina's face lit up. 'I got an idea,' she murmured. 'Hey, Mister Guard – watch this!'

She launched into a series of cartwheels and handsprings, tumbling her way down the gravel drive that led to the gate. The guard watched, open-mouthed. Then she leapt up on to a high stone wall, behind which the ground fell away steeply, and continued her tumbling.

'No!' said the guard. 'The wall is wet, you could slip – come down at once!'

'Not likely!' said Catarina, executing an extravagant somersault.

The guard rushed from his post towards her. Seizing their chance, the Tangshan Tigers ran through the gates and into the palace grounds.

'Good old Catarina!' said Shawn.

'Yes, she's amazing!' said Matt. He felt a rush of exhilaration as he raced down the wet, slippery grass towards the lake.

He could see Chang and Ryan on the

bridge ahead. They were only a few paces apart now. No other people were in view; evidently the heavy rain had driven the tourists away. Looking back, Matt saw that Catarina had given the guard the slip and was running fast to join them. The guard pursued her for a few paces, then gave up.

The Tangshan Tigers ran on to the bridge together. Chang and Ryan had stopped still and were eyeballing one another.

'Sifu,' said Matt. 'Is – is everything all right?'

Chang Sifu stood with his back to them. Without turning round, he said: 'Stay back.'

'Yes, get out of it, kids!' snapped Ryan. 'This is none of your business. Go back to school.'

'No!' said Matt. 'Not before we know what's going on.'

'Then I'll tell you,' said Ryan. 'I'm going to fight your teacher. And I'm going to win. It's not going to be pretty, so if you're determined to stay you better cover your eyes.'

'But why?' burst out Matt. 'Why would you want to fight Master Chang?'

For a moment Ryan seemed to lose something of his self-assurance. His eyes flicked to one side, not meeting Matt's, as if he felt guilty. He didn't reply, but Matt saw Ryan's face and neck turning red and blotchy, as if he was uncomfortable.

'You may intend to fight,' said Chang, 'but I will not. I come here to meet and talk. I do not wish to fight.'

'Scared, are you?' sneered Ryan. He was back to his arrogant self.

'I have no reason to fight you.'

'You'll have a reason in a minute or two. You'll be fighting for everything you stand for.'

'I do not think so.'

Ryan began to circle Chang menacingly. Chang moved with him, keeping his adversary face-on.

'There's no getting out of this, old man. My

client has paid me good money to fight you and win, so that's exactly what I'm going to do.'

So I was right! thought Matt. *He's being paid to do this – and it must be Drago that's paying him!*

'Do not be tempted by money,' said Chang. 'Let honour be your guide.'

Ryan's cheeks flushed an angry red. 'Enough!' He unleashed a karate kick that connected with a stone lion on the side of the bridge. The kick landed with such force that the lion's head snapped clean off and fell into the lake below.

Matt felt stunned. If that was what Ryan could do to a stone statue, what could he do to flesh and bone?

'Let's fight!' snarled Ryan.

He stopped circling and advanced straight towards Chang.

Matt saw Chang's body shift. Shoulders

square, feet apart, weight on back leg, toes, knees, hips and elbows pointing in the same direction. The centre line.

Chang was going to fight.

A flash of lightning lit up the sky. Almost immediately there was a crack of thunder as though the sky had split in two.

Ryan came forward fast. He launched a high, side-on kick aimed directly at Chang's jaw. With the slightest, most graceful of movements, Chang turned his body forty-five degrees. Ryan's kick met empty air. Chang was maintaining the centre line, Matt saw, controlling Ryan's line of attack. He pushed Ryan back a step.

Ryan spun round and tried again, this time with a fast flurry of kicks, aimed at Chang's head, chest, stomach and groin. Chang avoided them all, stepping back, slightly turning left and then right, fading away from the point of impact with millimetres to spare. Ryan was super-fast, but Chang made his movements look crude and clumsy.

Several times Ryan seemed to have left himself open to a counter-strike. *Go on*, Matt silently urged Chang, *hit him; counter-attack!* Yet their teacher did not strike back. His hands hung by his sides.

Ryan changed his tactics. Giving up on the kicks, he came in close and threw a series of chops and punches. Now Chang had to use his hands. He blocked Ryan's attacks deftly, without wasted effort, taking all the sting out of the blows. Ryan was grunting and snorting with the effort; Chang was perfectly silent.

'You can't keep this up much longer!' said Ryan. 'You know I'll get you in the end – and it's gonna hurt!'

He launched a sudden flurry of blows, driving forward.

Chang neutralized with a swift, double-handed

block that left Ryan reeling and off-balance. Chang could easily have landed a counter-punch or kick. Instead he pushed Ryan's shoulder, half-turning him round and making him stumble.

'Why don't you fight properly?' snarled Ryan. 'You're fighting like a girl!'

Matt saw Catarina's lips tighten.

'Well?' said Ryan. 'Afraid if you go for it you'll leave yourself open? I thought you were supposed to be a warrior!'

'You do not know what it means to be a warrior,' said Chang quietly.

Matt saw Ryan's eyes widen in rage. He rushed to the attack again, putting together a combination of furious kicks and spear-hand thrusts. Surely Chang couldn't evade his attacks forever?

'We've got to do something,' said Shawn. 'I can't watch this!' He began to run forward to go to Chang's aid.

Matt caught him by the arm. 'No! Chang told us to stay back.'

'Going to let a bunch of kids protect you, are you?' sneered Ryan.

'I've got an idea!' said Matt. 'Someone go and look for Li-Lian. We might need all the help we can get if things get any worse here.'

'I'll go!' said Catarina. She turned and ran through the driving rain.

Another flash of lightning; another crack of thunder. Chang and Ryan's tunics were sodden and clinging.

Still Ryan came on, and at last managed to get through Chang's guard with a two-fingered jab at the eyes. Chang turned a fraction too late; one finger only grazed its target, but the other struck him hard in the eye.

'No!' cried out Matt.

Chang moved backwards, one hand clutching his eye, the other held out in front of him to try and ward Ryan off.

A grim smile appeared on Ryan's lips. He had the upper hand now, and he knew it.

'This has gone too far!' said Olivier. 'We must do something. Can't we call the cops?'

'Sure thing,' said Shawn. He took out his phone. 'I've got all the emergency numbers for Beijing stored.' He spoke into the phone in Mandarin.

'No need for police,' said Chang, still trying to ward Ryan off one-handed.

'It'll be too late by the time they get here!' said Ryan grimly. 'You'd better call an ambulance instead.'

He knocked Chang's arm aside and landed a kick into Chang's ribs. Chang grunted. Ryan kicked again, this time aiming for the groin. Though half-blinded, Chang saw it in time and managed to turn aside. He took the force of the kick on the hip. He staggered, giving ground. And still Ryan came on.

Ryan had driven Chang perilously close to

the edge of the bridge. The parapet was low, and one more determined assault would knock Chang clean over it. The lake was far below and the water was not deep – serious injury was the very least Chang could expect.

Ryan launched another kick on Chang's blind side. It hit him in the chest and slammed him back against the parapet. *How can he fight when he can hardly see?* thought Matt desperately.

Chang took his hand away from his face – Matt glimpsed the red, puffy, closed eye beneath – and as Ryan threw himself forward for a final, decisive strike, Chang widened his stance to give himself better balance and deftly blocked the strike, knocking Ryan's arm up. He moved in and above and trapped Ryan in a tight neck-grip.

At once Matt saw the cleverness of Chang's strategy. Half-blinded, he couldn't match Ryan strike for strike; in a stand-up fight he would surely lose. But at close quarters, Ryan's advantage was neutralized.

Ryan was taken by surprise. He struggled, trying to break the grip, trying to throw Chang off-balance; but Chang, with his lower centre of gravity and wide-legged stance was the better balanced of the two. All his strength, all his energy was focused on the centre line, the area directly in front of him occupied by Ryan's body – and though Ryan was the bigger man, Chang was driving him backwards.

With his one free hand Ryan thudded punches into Chang's side. Chang seemed unaffected. He hooked his leg behind Ryan's and threw him. As Ryan fell, Chang shifted his grip so that Ryan twisted in mid-air and hit the ground face-first, with sickening force. Chang landed on top of him.

Ryan continued to struggle, attempting to throw Chang off. Chang got him in an armlock, securing Ryan's arm in the crook of his elbow, bending it across his back. Ryan yelped in pain.

'I do not wish to break your arm,' said Chang. 'Do not oblige me to do so.'

Ryan stopped struggling.

Matt let out a shaky sigh of relief. The fight was over.

He and the other Tigers approached the two men.

'Sifu – are you OK?' asked Shawn.

Chang looked at the Tangshan Tigers. 'I will be fine.'

Matt gazed down at Sensei Ryan, still lying face-down, his arm held in Chang's vice-like grip. 'Well?' he said. 'How much did Drago pay you for this?'

'Drago?' mumbled Ryan. 'It was nothing to do with Drago.'

'Oh, come on!' said Matt. 'We're not idiots, we know it was Drago –'

'You *are* idiots,' Ryan said. 'Do you honestly

think I'd take money or orders from a kid like Drago? I wish now I'd never . . . I was paid to challenge Master Chang in combat by –'

A ray of blue light hit Ryan in the chest. It was like a lightning strike. Chang released Ryan immediately but it was too late. Ripples of blue light shimmered over Ryan's body. His mouth opened; his body twitched convulsively. Matt watched in horror as the twitching stopped and Ryan slumped lifelessly to the ground.

THE FIGHT IN THE BOAT

'What the –' began Shawn.

'Has he been struck by lightning?' said Olivier.

'Not lightning. Get down!' said Chang sharply.

Their teacher was hit by another ray of blue light. His body stiffened and convulsed. Then he collapsed.

The Tangshan Tigers hit the deck. Fast.

Matt cautiously raised his head and looked in the direction the rays had come from. At the far end of the bridge stood three men.

They were dressed in black. One held a peculiar-looking weapon, like a cross between a gun and a movie camera. They had appeared as secretly and silently as snakes.

As *snakes*! Matt remembered Chang's mysterious warning about the sinister snake that could be deadly. Was this the threat he had meant? But who were these men?

'What about Master Chang?' asked Shawn. 'Is he OK?'

Chang lay on his side, knees drawn up to his chest. His eyes were closed and his face was waxy and pale.

Matt felt Chang's wrist. 'His pulse is beating. He's just unconscious.'

Olivier felt for Ryan's pulse. 'Ryan too,' he said.

'Must have been some sort of stun gun,' said Shawn. 'Zaps you with an electric shock strong enough to knock you out.'

'What's happened?' called an anguished voice.

It was Li-Lian running towards them with Catarina. She knelt by her grandfather and cradled his head in her hands.

'He's all right,' said Matt. 'Just stunned.'

'They knocked each other out?' asked Catarina.

'It's those men,' said Matt, pointing. The three men were walking purposefully along by the side of the lake now. 'They shot him with some kind of ray.'

Behind the men, Matt could see security guards talking into their walkie-talkies. They were hiding behind one of the palace gates and Matt realized that they didn't dare come near because of the stun guns. *Some security guards!* he thought.

'I'll call the police and an ambulance,' said Shawn, taking out his phone.

'And the men?' asked Olivier. 'I don't fancy being stunned by one of those guns.'

'We can't just let them get away,' said Matt.

'It's four against three, after all. We'll have to watch out for the stun gun, like you said – but if we can keep them busy here, it might be enough time for the police to get on the scene.'

'Good call,' said Catarina. 'Let's go!'

'You'd better stay with your grandfather, Li-Lian,' said Matt.

'Don't worry, Grandfather,' said Li-Lian, stroking the unconscious Chang's hair. 'The ambulance will be here soon.'

The Tangshan Tigers set off at a run, over the bridge and down the path that led to the shore of the lake. All four were good runners, especially Catarina and Olivier who set the pace, and they were soon gaining on the men in black. As he ran, Matt could see that the men stood beside a long, narrow boat, moored to a jetty.

One of the men shouted something to the other two, who immediately piled into the boat. The first man still stood on the jetty, untying the mooring rope.

Twenty metres to go.

The boat's engine started with a roar.

Ten metres to go.

The man on the jetty finished untying the rope. He jumped into the boat.

Five metres.

The boat began to move off, churning a creamy wake behind it.

'They've got away!' yelled Olivier.

'No, they haven't!' shouted Matt.

He ran down the jetty and took a flying leap. He landed with a thud in the middle of the boat, causing it to rock dangerously. The men in the boat grabbed the sides, shouting in alarm.

A moment later and the other Tigers leapt aboard too.

Gradually, the boat steadied. The men looked triumphant now. Gloating. Cruel.

'Thank you for dropping in,' said one, a tall thin man with a scar on his cheek.

As Matt watched, a wooden hatch door leading below deck was flung open and two more men stepped up. Too late, Matt realized that he had led the Tigers into a dangerous situation. Now there were five men on the deck – four of them young, strong Chinese men, the fifth older and more thickset, wearing a black velvet mask. They surrounded the Tangshan Tigers.

There was a long pause, broken only by the strong breeze and the spatter of rain upon the lake's surface. The water was getting choppier as the wind rose. The deck of the boat heaved beneath them.

'What shall we do with them?' said the man with a scar.

'Let's give them the same medicine we gave the martial arts teachers!' said another. He was a broad-shouldered, athletic man with a goatee beard.

The man in the velvet mask nodded. 'Good

idea,' he said with relish. 'They are young, less strong than fully grown adults. It will be an interesting experiment.'

There was something familiar about his voice. Matt had heard it before, he was sure of that. But where? Who was behind that mask?

There was another flash of lightning and peal of thunder. The wind was wild, blowing ice-cold rain into their faces.

'Which one should we do first, boss?' said the man holding the stun gun.

'Wait,' said Matt. If he kept talking they might have a chance to think of a way out. 'I don't get it. What have we done to you?'

'Ah, you do not know? Then perhaps this will refresh your memory.'

The man slowly peeled off his mask.

The Tangshan Tigers gasped.

'Sang!' said Matt.

The face behind the mask – a square, strong face, with cold eyes and a hint of cruelty about the mouth – belonged to the man who had once kidnapped Li-Lian and threatened her with death; who hated Chang Sifu for preventing him from getting rich from the oil deposits secretly buried under the Great Wall of China. He had tried to crush Li-Lian and her grandfather and the Tangshan Tigers beneath a million tons of rock.

Sang nodded. 'Yes, it's me. Last time you derailed my plans. This time I have you at my mercy.'

'But there's nothing you could gain by harming us!' said Olivier.

'You are wrong,' said Sang with an icy smile. 'I will gain my revenge.'

Keep him talking, thought Matt. 'So it was you who paid Ryan to fight Chang?' he asked. 'Why did you do that?'

'I wanted to see Chang beaten – humiliated – and for him to know it was all my doing. But Ryan wasn't good enough! No matter. I

127

haven't finished with Chang yet. By striking at you children I can hurt him badly. And he will know — because he knows the kind of man I am — that my revenge will not stop there!'

Matt had got the Tangshan Tigers into this mess. It was up to him to get them out. He could feel a plan forming in his head.

The wind had risen still higher and the boat was rocking violently.

'Remember,' Matt said quietly to the Tigers, 'balance is the key to everything. Right?'

He saw comprehension dawn in the Tigers' eyes, as they watched the men stumble about on the heaving deck.

'Yup,' said Catarina softly. 'Got it.'

'Enough talking!' said Sang. 'To business. Ladies first, I think!' He pointed at Catarina and rapped out an order in Mandarin.

The man with the stun gun pointed it at Catarina. But the boat was pitching so much that his aim wavered up and down.

'Now!' shouted Matt.

He stepped forward and lashed out with a high axe kick, knocking the stun gun from the man's hands. The man staggered, cursing, scrabbling for the fallen weapon in the bottom of the boat.

The Tangshan Tigers leapt into action simultaneously. Each targeted a man.

Catarina went for the man with the scar on his cheek. He lashed out at her, but she easily dodged his fists. She caught one of his hands and spun him round and, as he staggered, a simple push was enough to send him over the side of the boat.

'Enjoy your swim!' she called.

The man with the goatee had grabbed Shawn by the shoulders, stumbling as he did so. Shawn was already turning into the man's body, bending, pulling on the man's arm so that he rolled over Shawn's back. The man flew in an arc and splashed into the water.

Olivier went straight for his man. Off-balance, the man swung his fists wildly. Moving his body, maintaining the centre line, Olivier evaded the blows and neatly caught the man's wrist. He turned it. The man howled in pain. He had to move his arm in the direction Olivier was twisting it, or his wrist would be snapped. Olivier forced him to bend right over the side of the boat and, with a final twist of the arm, flipped him into the water.

Matt's opponent had grabbed the stun gun again – but as he attempted to raise it, Matt hit it with an unexpected reverse kick and it flew out of his hands. The man hissed and came for Matt. Matt met him straight-on. He visualized his centre line, directly in front of him, exactly where his opponent stood. Despite the rocking of the boat, Matt was able to hold his balance, keeping his weight on the back foot. Chang's training had paid off!

The man aimed a roundhouse punch, which

Matt blocked, double-handed, with all the
weight of his body behind it. The force of the
counter sent the man reeling back. Matt still
came forward. A spear-hand thrust to the belly
doubled the man up; a high, straight kick to
the jaw sent him flying over the side of the
boat to join his fellows in the freezing water.

'Tigers rule!' cried Catarina.

All their enemies had been pitched overboard
– except for Sang, who'd stood at the back of
the boat away from the fighting. His face was
grim. But he made no move to attack.

His men were struggling in the water. They
cried out as they tried to grab on to the sides
of the boat – but in the heaving water they
couldn't get a grip. They fell back, their heads
disappearing beneath the waves, to reappear
further away from the boat, panic etched on
their faces.

With a shock, Matt realized they couldn't
swim.

'They are drowning!' said Sang, looking directly at Matt.

'We have to get them out,' said Matt to the other Tigers. 'Otherwise —'

'They tried to zap us with a stun gun!' said Catarina.

'But we can't let them drown,' said Matt.

'Seems a bit severe,' agreed Olivier, as he came to stand beside Matt.

Matt turned to look at Sang. 'I don't trust him or his men, but we can't stand back and watch people drown. Right now they need us more than we need them, they'd be stupid to fight.'

Sang gave an insincere smile. 'I won't move a muscle,' he promised. Matt had no idea if he could trust Sang, but what choice did he have?

'You guys help the men,' Matt said to the Tangshan Tigers; 'I'd better stay with Sang.'

'Let's do it!' said Shawn.

The men were now too far from the boat to

be hauled in – the friends would have to dive in and get them. The Tigers slipped their shoes off.

'We're coming to get you!' Catarina called out. 'But don't give us no trouble or you gonna regret it!'

She dived in and the other Tigers followed suit. Just as Matt saw Catarina reach the first man, he felt a tap on the shoulder.

He turned to see the squat, thickset figure of Sang behind him. Sang grinned, revealing filthy yellow, crooked teeth.

'I lied,' he said, shrugging. Then he aimed a karate chop at the side of Matt's neck.

Sang was fast.

But Matt's reactions were faster.

Instinctively, he turned his body – he felt the wind of the blow pass over his head. Carried on by his own momentum, Sang plunged forward and crashed into Matt.

Matt grasped Sang round his thick waist. If he could throw him . . . but Sang was too big, too heavy, too strong. He stood firm. His fist crashed into Matt's stomach, making him cry out in pain.

Matt knew he couldn't take many more hits like that. At the same time, he felt a slight shift in Sang's stance – aiming that blow had altered his centre of gravity. He pushed hard and felt Sang give ground – he could not fully regain his balance. Matt hooked his leg behind Sang's, just as he'd seen Chang do to Ryan earlier, at the same time driving his weight forward.

Sang bellowed in rage as he felt himself going over. He clutched despairingly at Matt, trying to take him down with him – but Matt slipped neatly from his grasp.

Sang hit the deck. Matt placed his foot on the man's neck.

'Don't move,' he said. 'Or I'll break your neck.'

'You would not do such a thing!' said Sang between gritted teeth.

'Wouldn't I?' said Matt quietly. 'Want to put it to the test?'

Sang lay very still. Of course, Matt would never have been able to break a man's neck in cold blood. But Sang didn't know that.

The other Tangshan Tigers were climbing aboard again, pulling the bedraggled men with them. All the fight had gone out of the men. Once aboard the boat they sat shivering on the wooden seats, teeth chattering. Matt and his friends weren't going to take any more chances; Catarina found a coil of rope and they tied them together, pulling the rope tight.

The Tangshan Tigers were in much better spirits.

'Hey, you sorted out Sang!' Shawn said to Matt. 'Way to go, dude!'

'Well, someone had to . . .' said Matt.

'Now what?' said Catarina. 'Anyone know how to steer this boat?'

'*Moi*,' said Olivier. 'I've been sailing with my dad loads of times.'

He took the wheel and steered the boat back towards the shore.

'Look,' said Catarina, pointing. 'The cops have arrived.'

Matt saw several police officers waiting on the jetty. They must have come in response to Shawn's call and been directed here by Li-Lian.

'Hello!' said Olivier in his most charming manner as the boat nosed into the jetty. 'I wonder if you could help us? We have some gentlemen here for you to take care of – they tried to shoot us with an electric stun gun. Look, it's here in the boat.'

'We saw,' said the chief officer, a tall man in a peaked cap. 'We will take care of this now.' Then he spoke in Mandarin to the men in black. They sullenly climbed up on to the jetty.

Matt took his foot from Sang's neck and stepped back. Sang got stiffly to his feet. As he

climbed out of the boat, he turned and
directed a look of such hatred at Matt that he
felt a shiver run down his spine.

'I do not forget,' Sang said.

Matt did his best to look unconcerned. He
and the other Tigers also climbed ashore.

'Hey, where'd the others go?' said Catarina
suddenly. 'Look – there's no one on the
bridge!'

Matt saw the bridge was empty.

'They are safe,' said the chief officer, who
appeared to be the only one who spoke
English. 'They have been taken to Kunming
District Hospital. It is not far.'

'Is it OK if we go there?' Matt asked. 'If you
want to speak to us as witnesses later, you can
easily find us – we're students at the Beijing
International Academy.'

'I know,' said the chief officer. 'Chang Sifu
told us.'

It was evident from the way he said the

name that he knew who Chang was and had a great respect for him.

Two policemen took Sang by an arm each and led him towards the palace. His dripping henchmen were also escorted away.

Matt felt a throb of relief at seeing Sang removed from the scene. The authorities would deal with him – and hopefully he would never have to see the man again. Sang wasn't important any more. The really important thing was that Chang Sifu was safe.

'Come on,' he said. 'It's not over yet. Let's go and see how Chang is.'

AFTERMATH

Chang was in a private room at the hospital.
A nurse showed them to the room and tapped
on the door.

'Come in,' came Chang's voice, sounding
lively and alert.

Chang was sitting up in bed, wearing a
green hospital gown. A surgical patch covered
his right eye. A single lotus flower in a bowl of
water stood on the bedside table.

Li-Lian sat beside him, holding his hand.

The Tigers lined up by the side of the bed,
paying Chang the traditional sign of respect,

placing their right fists into open left hands in front of their chests.

'How are you feeling?' asked Matt.

'Being hit by that bolt of electricity – that had to hurt!' said Shawn.

'It has left me weak. And fight took its toll as well. But these things will pass.' He smiled. "All things must pass," as the great Lao-Tze said.'

'I have told you, how foolish to get into a fight at your age!' Li-Lian scolded him affectionately.

'And the eye?' asked Catarina.

'Only a scratch. It will heal.'

'We're glad you're OK, Sifu,' said Matt. 'You know it was Sang behind the attack.'

Chang nodded.

'He's been arrested now,' said Matt.

Chang looked at Matt shrewdly. 'Am I to guess that Tangshan Tigers had something to do with this outcome?'

'Er, yeah, we were kind of involved . . .'

'You have done well. Today you faced a dangerous enemy. I did not want you to run this risk. But, as always, Tangshan Tigers make me proud! There should be no more trouble from Sang. He will go to prison for long time.'

Matt hoped so. He found himself remembering Sang's last words to him, spoken with a deadly seriousness: *I do not forget.*

There was another knock on the door. Matt turned to see Sensei Ryan enter. Immediately Matt felt hostile. He clenched his fists and moved to stand between Chang and Ryan. So did the other Tigers.

'What's he doing here?' said Catarina.

But Ryan did not appear to have come looking for trouble. He moved stiffly. His eyes were downcast and he looked humble, chastened.

Chang motioned the Tangshan Tigers to one side.

'Sifu,' said Ryan. 'I have come to apologize.'

He bowed awkwardly. Matt saw his hands were handcuffed behind his back.

'You are under arrest?' asked Chang.

'Yes. The police found out I was paid by Sang to attack you. But I wanted to let you know – I didn't really do it for the money. I just had to know who was better.'

'I understand,' said Chang.

'I did it for the honour of saying I had fought the greatest living master. My reasons were not pure, and I am sorry I accepted money when I had no quarrel with you. But still, I am proud to say we fought. And though I lost, even to lose to such a master is an honour.'

He bowed.

To Matt's surprise, Chang got stiffly out of bed. Li-Lian ran to take his arm. He faced Ryan; then he too bowed.

'It was an honour to fight you too,' he said.

'You have great spirit and ability. You will put them to better use in time.'

'Thanks,' said Ryan, almost in a whisper.

A uniformed police officer, who had been waiting discreetly at the door, stepped into the room and tapped Ryan on the arm. Ryan followed him out.

'We should go too, Grandfather,' said Li-Lian. 'Let you rest.'

Chang eased himself back on to the bed. 'Li-Lian, stay and talk with me awhile. You others – thank you for all you have done. Truly, it is appreciated. But you should go back to Academy now.'

'I guess we'd better,' said Matt. 'And find out what sort of trouble we're in!'

They caught a bus back to the Academy. On the way, Matt said: 'I wish we could do something about Master Chang and Li-Lian – I mean, it doesn't seem right that they have to go back and live in that shack on the hillside.'

'We'll have to see what we can do,' said Olivier thoughtfully.

As they entered the Beijing Academy the electronic wind-chimes tinkled to announce their arrival. Two security guards pounced on them.

'So there you are! Mr Wu will see you in his office. Immediately!'

Mr Wu sat behind his enormous, highly polished desk, regarding them sternly through his glittering spectacles.

'Stand there – in a line – on the carpet. Hands behind backs!' he barked. 'You four have been absent from school without leave, you have broken bounds, you have told lies about non-existent Outreach Programme! What have you to say for yourselves?'

'About the Outreach Programme,' said Olivier, 'we were thinking that was a really good idea, and maybe in future the Academy could –'

Mr Wu banged a fist on the desk. 'Do not add insolence to your crimes! What you have done is punishable by expulsion! I must consider the options – but rest assured you will not simply get away with disobedience on this scale. What would my fellow principals say if they learned that students in my Academy made holiday whenever they wished, without my permission?'

'May I ask a question, sir?' asked Matt softly.

Mr Wu stared at him. A bright-red spot appeared on each of his cheeks.

'I am not here to answer your questions –' he began.

But Matt continued: 'What would your fellow principals say if they learned that this school doesn't have a single martial arts teacher on the staff? I mean, this Academy prides itself on martial arts . . .'

'What do you mean?' said Mr Wu. 'We have Sensei Ryan, a first-rate instructor –'

'Not any more,' said Shawn. He pulled his BlackBerry from his pocket and clicked for the latest headlines on the Internet. 'You see here, sir, where it says Ryan has been arrested –'

'What?' Mr Wu snatched the BlackBerry from Shawn. 'Martial arts teacher arrested,' he read aloud in a wondering tone, 'for his part in a revenge plot to beat up his predecessor?'

The colour drained from Mr Wu's cheeks. Without a word, he handed the BlackBerry back to Shawn. He went and stood by the window, looking out.

'It won't look too good if we don't have a martial arts teacher,' said Catarina. 'If we don't give Chang his job back it might even look like we're kind of on Ryan's side, you know?'

Mr Wu was silent for a moment. Then he

cleared his throat and turned to face the
Tangshan Tigers.

'Of course, it goes without saying that I
should be only too glad to have Master Chang
back after his, er –' he gave a small cough –
'after his vacation. I thought that too obvious
to mention.'

'And he has a granddaughter to support, you
know,' said Matt. He could see that Mr Wu
would do anything to keep this scandal as low-
key as possible; it was worth risking one more
bit of cheek. 'Perhaps his salary . . .?'

'Yes, yes,' said Mr Wu testily. 'It will be
increased, naturally. Doubled.'

'And about the Outreach Programme,' said
Olivier. 'Helping local schools in the
community, you know –'

'I will consider it,' said Mr Wu. 'Er . . .' He
cleared his throat. 'In the circumstances . . . since
you have alerted me to this situation, we will
say no more about punishment. You may go!'

Outside in the corridor, Catarina turned a celebratory cartwheel.

'Mission accomplished!' grinned Shawn.

The Tangshan Tigers high-fived one another, laughing.

'Wait a minute!' said Shawn. 'I'm going to go get something.'

He hurried away and returned a few moments later with the Electro-Hound.

'What's that for?' asked Matt.

Shawn led them to a nearby changing room where a number of training tops were hanging from a row of hooks. He riffled through them, then activated the Electro-Hound and let it sniff at one of the tops.

'What are you doing?' said Catarina.

'We're going to track down Carl! Don't you think he'll be delighted to learn Ryan's gone and Chang Sifu's coming back?'

'I bet he will!' said Matt.

The Electro-Hound emitted a whirring

noise. Its eyes glowed red. Shawn put it on the ground and it immediately began to race away, snuffling as it went.

The Tangshan Tigers ran along behind it, laughing and whooping.

Just round the corner they met Andrei Drago, who stared at them in surprise.

'Hey, what's going on? What are you all so excited about?'

'Nothing!' said Matt. 'I mean, everything! Just pleased, pleased about the way things are turning out – pleased you're on the team, mate! Everyone deserves a chance.'

He slapped Drago on the back and ran on after the others.

Drago and his father didn't seem such a big deal any more. OK, so Old Man Drago must have pulled a few strings to get his son into the school, and probably had exerted a bit of influence to get him into the martial arts team. But the Tangshan Tigers had faced much bigger crooks than that. Compared to Sang and his gang, the Dragos weren't even on the starting line.

Matt leapt and punched the air as he caught up with the Electro-Hound and the Tigers.

'We've done it again!' he said. 'Another adventure for the Tangshan Tigers!'

'All we got to do now is get you back in the team,' said Catarina.

'Do you think I'll get back in?' Matt would have to wait a bit longer for his injury to heal, but after that . . .?

'Sure to!' said Catarina.

'Bound to!' said Shawn.

'Certain to!' said Olivier.

Things are looking good, thought Matt. And they were only going to get better.

Masters of Martial Arts
Fighters of Crime
together they're the

Matt

Shawn

TANGSHAN TIGERS

Catarina

puffin.co.uk

Olivier

TANGSHAN TIGERS

Shawn Hung

Age: 12

Nationality: Chinese-American

Sport: Judo

Special Skill: The *ko soto gari* throw

Strengths: Extremely well balanced on his feet, judo is the perfect sport for Shawn. And with a new gadget for every adventure, Shawn is a complete techno-whizz when it comes to tackling crime.

Weaknesses: Shawn can bear grudges easily and his loyalty to family and friends can conflict with his crime-stopping instincts.

Join the Team and Win a Prize!

Do YOU have what it takes to be a Tangshan Tiger?

Answer the questions below for the chance to win an exclusive Tangshan Tigers kit bag. Kit bag contains T-shirt, headband and cloth badge.*

1. What is the Chinese term for 'training hall'?

   a) Kwoon   **b)** Karateka **c)** Kufu

2. Catarina's specialty is capoeira. Which country does this martial art come from?

   a) Britain   **b)** Bolivia   **c)** Brazil

3. In Karate, a sequence of movements performed without a partner is called kata.

   a) True   **b)** False

Send your answers in to us with your name, date of birth and address. Each month we will put every correct answer in a draw and pick out one lucky winner.

Tangshan Tigers Competition, Puffin Marketing, 80 Strand, London WC2R 0RL

Closing date is 31 August 2010.